the Whitsun Daughters

the Whitsun Daughters

CARRIE MESROBIAN

DUTTON BOOKS

DUTTON BOOKS
An imprint of Penguin Random House LLC, New York

Copyright © 2020 by Carrie Mesrobian

Penguin supports copyright. Copyright fuels creativity, encourages diverse voices, promotes free speech, and creates a vibrant culture. Thank you for buying an authorized edition of this book and for complying with copyright laws by not reproducing, scanning, or distributing any part of it in any form without permission. You are supporting writers and allowing Penguin to continue to publish books for every reader.

Dutton is a registered trademark of Penguin Random House LLC.

Visit us online at penguinrandomhouse.com

Library of Congress Cataloging-in-Publication Data is available.
Printed in the United States of America

ISBN 9780735231955

1 3 5 7 9 10 8 6 4 2

Design by Anna Booth

Text set in Adobe Jenson Pro

For my mother, and her mothers before her

All the stream that's roaring by
Came out of a needle's eye;
Things unborn, things that are gone,
From needle's eye still goad it on.

—William Butler Yeats, "A Needle's Eye"

Prologue

Across the sea from where I was born, what was Ó *Cathaiseach* is faded away to the mere unmusical *Casey*; my kin, Ó *Murchadha*, descended from the sea wolf, in this place shriveled like a salted snail: *Murphy*. According to the pages in their Bible and the blessing of a traveling priest who left after breakfast the following morning, I am a Ganey (once Ó *Geigheannaigh*, alas).

They did not before, but now, how names especially vex me.

I am not a Ganey, and I only belonged to Patrick Casey for a time. I must be a Murphy, then. Though truly my end would shame the sea wolf.

I am caught here. Remaining was my choice. This mostly soothes me. But time has become peculiar. When once hours flowed from day to night in measured drams, now ungainly bits catch in time's spout, slowing a gush to a trickle. Nights, I glide above treetops over the lines the living have drawn (and redrawn, soaked with their blood and sweat and rage, traded and cut to suit, named and renamed), until the morning sun swells over fields bristling with growth, and for a moment I cannot remember who I was.

But I always come back to myself. And to the fact of the names, too: dripping with meaning one minute, wrung dry of all sense the next.

The names of my girls are never in my mouth. I think of them as Patrick might, in the colors of horses. The eldest a golden palomino, prancing, arrogant; the middle child a flossy white unicorn, shimmering in her slightness; the youngest a cautious dark bay whose eyes are always watching. She does not see me; at times I wish she could. A living body contains such fires, and my body, so long underground, is become earth itself, not merely beneath it. Sweet woodruff and gentian, ferns and milkweed, the orange fringe of mushrooms, a sturdy oak: what was me became as something whispered in the dark, a secret turned up like a clutch of newborn rabbits under a plow. I am naught more than the sound of a pipe pitching out notes before a revel. All angles, yet no set size. Only nights when the moon turns its face can I move freely, traveling above rooftops and along windowsills until dawn calls me back.

I am no longer a creature, yet my habits remain. My desires, still the old ones. Lurking amidst the brush, watching squirrels collect acorns and deer drink from puddles. Watching my girls. I am allowed pleasure here, too, despite the warnings of the Bible my mother loved so well. It is pleasure, and my delight, to see my girls, their skin supple and sweating, their mouths eating, their fists clamping over their hips as their legs bend and stretch over the earth. The work of bodies never ends. I particularly like their hair, how it grows long and shaggy until lopped off by one of their mothers, the priestly one whose thoughts swirl like perfume in lilac time; she finds such joyful thrift in snipping the little girls' tresses. Where I had watched Patrick feed Arthur Ganey's horses is now a kitchen with an unlikely polished floor; over what was dirt and hay, the priestly mother sweeps up the girls' lost tresses—gold, white, mahogany. The priestly one's sister, a midwife, makes each daughter gulp down spoonfuls of castor and fish oil; one year, they each suffered needle jabs, given for their own good. Their tears brimmed and they winced under the puncture, their betrayed howls ringing out through the open windows.

The palomino girl loves so harshly; she sees everything as a prize to be won or lost. The unicorn girl's love ripples uncontained; her soul is flimsy, easily stained by sadness or goaded into laughter. The dark bay foal, who has since become steady on her feet in a manner that I envy, rushes through the brush. She is a thirsty creature. I ache when I see her touch the cool water at the bottom of the ravine where Patrick liked to wash.

A house helmed by two sisters, and their three daughters. The mothers' love, borne of their sister pact, has made a world where no men ever deigned to rule. The daughters' love sometimes passes heavy, a pail of milk to a waiting hand; other times it passes light, easy, a hairbrush before a Sunday service. It is most visible in their hands: what they make and toss away, what they strive to hold. I watch for restfulness. The after hours of tables cleared and dishes washed and floors swept and pencils and needles jabbing at paper and cloth; here their thick love dreams and wraps over each other, like hair in a braid. This reminds me of my own sister, and I recall my beating heart, strong beneath my chemise, galloping in grief for her. I think of my own hair—long gone, a cat's cradle for the faeries—and the relief of unwinding it each night, the burden heavy no more. I think of my own hands and what they learned about desire.

How quickly everything in God's world disintegrates. Everything but the loneliness of young women.

Chapter One

"Okay, you know what's metal?" Wade asked. "An angel comes down to earth, smashes a guitar against the ground, and a whole shitload of bats flies out."

"What's *metal* about that?" Lilah asked. "The guitar? Is that even actually made of metal? Is it an acoustic guitar? Because those aren't metal at all." She laughed and poked Wade in the ribs, which made him jerk the whole truck, slamming Daisy into Poppy, who groaned and put on her sunglasses.

"This is so stupid," Poppy said.

"I think it's kind of funny," Daisy offered.

"Lilah's turn," Wade said.

Lilah pushed her hair out of her eyes while she thought. They sat four across in Wade Dunedin's truck: Poppy at the opposite window, then Daisy, then Lilah smashed against Wade, who took up a third of the cab. Daisy pressed her knees together, tense and sweaty. Sometimes, Lilah was unaware of how long she took to say something, even in a normal conversation, not a game like this one. Even on regular days when they weren't coming back from a funeral.

"Jesus, Lilah!" Poppy said. "It's not like it's fucking astrophysics! Just make something up!"

"I'm thinking!" Lilah shouted.

"Good things take time," said Wade as he steered his truck out onto Warren Street, diverging from the convoy of other funeral goers.

Daisy agreed. She wished Poppy would stop being such a bitch. Half an hour earlier, Wade had been in tears in the pew next to them, watching his best friend, Hugh Isherwood, and Hugh's older brother, Brian, set flowers beside a blown-up photo of their mother, Evie Isherwood. The whole service had been nonstop bawling, which Daisy expected. But seeing Evie Isherwood's younger son in tears had never been anything she expected to see in her entire life of knowing him: Hugh and his handsome, brash pride, whether they were in the hallway at school or running along the dirt roads off Old Blackmun Road. She herself had not cried at all.

"All right," said Lilah. "I've got one. Wouldn't it be, don't you think, so very metal if, say, an eagle swooped down from the sky just as a bear was swiping a fish out of a river and poked out its eye?"

"Whose eye?" Poppy asked. "The bear's or the fish's?"

"It's pretty metal either way," Wade said.

"Poking out a fish eye isn't metal," Poppy said. "You dissect a perch in ninth grade; the eye pops out like a little ball of rubber cement. It's gross, not gory."

Daisy thought Poppy had a point, but she knew Wade was just trying to be nice to them, and there were plenty of people in the town of Hogestyn who didn't bother. The Whitsun girls were more accustomed to giving help than receiving it, but not today. Wade had invited Poppy and her mother, Carna, to sit in their pew; when Daisy and Lilah trailed behind with their mother, Violet, who, though she wasn't in charge of the service in this church, had been with the Isherwoods helping out behind the scenes all morning, Wade stood up and ushered them all farther down the row. He handed Violet a program and offered sticks of spearmint gum and pushed hymnals toward them when it was time to sing; he put his arm along the back row of the wooden pew. He did all this, though Poppy made it clear she didn't like him, and Lilah acted like a space case the whole time, and Violet murmured little dorky *hmms* and *ahhs* while the pastor spoke, as if she were being talked to, singularly, and Carna looked sea green, like one of her migraines was coming on. Wade asked his father to drive Carna and Violet home once they were done collecting the flowers for the family, and Wade took on their daughters as his own responsibility.

"What kind of bear should it be?" Lilah asked.

"Who cares?" Poppy said. "They're all nine-hundred-pound carnivores. They're all scary as hell."

"A full-grown bear, though," Wade added, turning toward the SuperAmerica across from the Dollar Tree, where the guy selling fireworks under a big tarp in the parking lot was doing a brisk business despite the ungodly heat. It was the last week in June, and he'd been there two weeks. Poppy lowered her sunglasses and muttered something snobby about the people lining up to buy sparklers and spinners; she disapproved of fireworks.

"Make it a polar bear," Daisy said, feeling that she could use a blast of the arctic right now.

"Why are we stopping?" Poppy snapped.

"Eagles and polar bears are in the same ecosystem," Lilah said. "So that would work, I think. Poppy, can you look it up?"

Poppy didn't answer, though she was scrolling through her messages, and obviously had enough bars. Daisy marveled at how Poppy could be so mean and get away with it. It was probably because everyone thought she was so beautiful. But Daisy had never seen this. Poppy was tall and her body was strong and sure in lots of places, slight in others. But her thighs were thick from swimming, her calves long but not especially curved, her nose was too snubbed, her skin prone to breakouts. Even her blond hair, thick as the pages of a textbook, was starting to darken as Carna's had. Poppy's beauty was not constant; it was far from irresistible.

For Daisy, who had spent her entire life observing her older cousin, living with her as a sister, sharing bathtubs and bedtime stories and closets of hand-me-down clothes, the truth was that people were captivated by Poppy merely because she intended them to be. This was because Poppy, more than anything, was smart. She was calm yet sharp, poised but ultracompetent. When Violet and little Lilah had come to live with Violet's older sister, Carna, Poppy was five, and Daisy still in her mother's belly. The story their mothers liked to tell was how that first night, when she had learned that not just Lilah would be moving into her room, but another little baby, Poppy cried and cried. Her attic domain in the house on Old Blackmun Road, painted sweet yellows and lavenders, would be invaded by two others. But the tears didn't last. Soon she ruled over Lilah's wayward naughtiness and delighted in ordering her younger cousin's days with picture books and cups of carrot sticks and laces of yarn they held between their fingers in complicated twists. Once Daisy came along, Poppy was as inevitable as a brick wall. A force of discipline beside Lilah's silliness, a bright line underscoring the wavy haze of Violet's fuzzy Unitarian theology and the thick slap of Carna's blood-and-guts reality as a nurse-midwife.

It was within these competing realms that Daisy had grown up, and this entire summer, she found herself running from them toward the creek at the bottom of the ravine behind their house every single morning. With the return of an all-knowing Poppy from her first year of college, there was no room in the Whitsun house for anything beyond blatant disobedience or bland compliance. The house was stuffed with opinions and proclamations and defensiveness for any given stance; Violet wanted to endlessly discuss these differences, while Carna worked to tamp down rage. The past year had been difficult, sure, but the return of the eldest Whitsun girl, who couldn't stop complaining about the slow internet and shit cell reception, brought with it more tension and conflict than her absence had.

Wade parked at the SuperAmerica and left the truck running

so the air-conditioning stayed on. "You want something to drink?" he asked, and while Daisy was thirsty, it seemed like he was only really asking Lilah.

"Apple juice?" Lilah said.

"You got it." He slammed the driver's door and the whole truck trembled.

"What the fuck?" Poppy said. "I can't *believe* this shit! We're what? Fifteen minutes from home, but he has to stop to get something to drink *now*?"

"You're such a Crabby Abby," Lilah said.

Poppy sighed and kept texting. Daisy cracked her neck. Even without Wade in the cab, it was still cramped. She wished she could take down her hair; the bobby pins were jabbing into her scalp. But Poppy had forced updos on all of them, including Carna, who always wore her hair loose; undoing all of Poppy's careful work right now would annoy her even more.

"What is taking him so fucking long?" Poppy hissed. "There's barely anyone even here!"

"Who are you texting?" Lilah asked.

"Nobody." Daisy glanced at Poppy's phone screen: a blue background with a graphic of a glum-looking woman moping over a block of text full of long chemical-sounding words she didn't recognize.

"God, Daisy." Poppy tipped the phone away. "Mind your business already."

"Is it your mom? Or our mom?" Lilah continued.

"No. Why do you care?"

"I don't know!" Lilah said. "Just wondering! Maybe they needed something; Aunt Carna was getting a headache and—"

"Jesus!" Poppy scowled. "She has *medication* for that; she just needs to *take it*. It sucks, but she doesn't need me to be involved. What do you expect me to do about any of it?"

"Nothing, obviously," Lilah said. "I'm just asking. Wondering. Can't we talk? Tell each other things?"

"I didn't realize we were allowed to talk about things that aren't metal."

"We can talk about anything you want," Lilah said. "What did you think about the funeral?"

"I don't need to talk about that, either."

"Did you talk to Hugh at all?"

"I said hello to him."

"So did everyone else," Daisy said.

"Why do I have to talk to him so much more than you guys, then?"

Lilah twitched, scratching at her upper arm, where a bruise threaded with little bits of red was blooming under the sleeve of her dress.

"Um, his mother died," Lilah said, her voice low. Daisy felt her sister's body cinch, and she wondered where the bruise had come from. Lilah had never been the rough-and-tumble type.

"Don't act like I owe him something," Poppy said. She clicked something on her phone, and grinned. "We weren't married. Fucking hell."

"We grew up with him," Lilah said. "His whole family. It's not just that you went out with him for a while. That's not what I'm saying. We're neighbors."

"Look," Poppy said, putting down her phone. "I know all that. I do. But just because his mother died doesn't mean I suddenly feel different about him and what he did. He's not suddenly forgiven because there was a death in the family and . . ." She trailed off and began digging in her handbag.

A second later, Wade popped back behind the wheel with a giant cup of Coke. He handed Lilah a bottle of apple juice and Daisy again felt squashed against her family, "Any other stops before home?"

"Can you stop at Marshall's, please," Poppy said, sealing gloss on her lips.

"What are we doing there?" Wade asked.

"We're not doing anything," Poppy said. "You guys go home; I'll catch up later."

"What about the reception?" Wade was incredulous.

"I'll get a ride, don't worry," Poppy said.

Wade sucked on his Coke, reversing the truck with his right arm spread around Lilah, who rolled the condensation from her juice bottle between her palms and against her neck. All week, the temperatures had been in the upper nineties; it had been the hottest summer on record, everyone said, along with a short, nonexistent spring. No rain, no April showers. Just sun and heat, beating everyone down into a torpor. All along Old Blackmun Road, the corn sprouts were defeated in dry brown fields; here in town, the heat rose in witchy glimmers off the asphalt.

A block from Marshall's, Wade stopped at a light and Poppy said, "Right here's fine!" She jumped out, rushing through the crosswalk in her stacked black sandals, her long tan legs flashing as she sprinted toward the restaurant, where someone was waving to her from a patio table. Daisy immediately slid into the vacated spot.

"Who the fuck's she meeting?" Wade asked as they waited for the light to change.

"Probably Perry Coughlin," Lilah said while lazily shaking up her juice.

"Fucking cake-eater," Wade grumbled. The light turned green and he floored it. "What the fuck's he doing back?"

"He's lifeguarding at the Y this summer," Daisy said. She and Poppy had seen him at lap swim last week; Daisy waited forever while they talked on the pool deck.

"That fucking kid," Wade said, exiting off the ramp to the highway. "Annoys the piss out of me."

"He's two years older than you," Lilah said. "How can he be a kid?"

Wade shook his head. The mood in the truck was now sour. Even Lilah trying to resume the whole that-is-so-metal conversation didn't help. While she didn't care that Poppy ditched them—Poppy's absence this past year had been something she had very easily, and happily, adjusted to—Daisy still felt the weight of the day pressing on her. She had never been to a funeral before; she had never seen so many people she knew crying at one time. But there was something unreal about the funeral: Mrs. Isherwood was dead, but there was no coffin, no body. Just a picture of her in a red shirt, with red lips, her blond hair curling down her shoulders, gold necklaces glittering around her collarbone. Daisy had worked for Mrs. Isherwood last summer at the pick-your-own berry patch she ran, and she would have worked for her again, if not for the car accident that left her brain dead this March. After a lot of tests and family fighting, she was removed from life support a few weeks ago; the berries, untended, grew wayward and were now rotting atop the straw they'd carefully pitched over them last fall. Mr. Isherwood told neighbors to pick what they wanted; he didn't care. Daisy picked a bucket but couldn't bring herself to eat them.

Lilah cracked open her juice and began gulping it until it splattered onto the front of her yellow dress—another thing Poppy disliked, but Lilah refused to wear black for any reason and her updo was her only concession to Poppy's sense of propriety.

"Easy does it, Jesus!" Wade said, laughing.

"It's so good, though!" Lilah said, wiping her mouth. Instantly, the mood in the cab changed back to good. Lilah's powers in situations like this always fascinated Daisy, especially since most of the year her sister had been in a gloomy funk. Moping around, sleeping constantly, crying in the bathtub with the door locked so no one could pee, doctor appointments and hushed conversations, arguments between her and Violet that stopped whenever Daisy came into the room. Refusing to take even ibuprofen when she had bad cramps, and just silently weeping as she lay on the sofa, insisting she was fine and it was natural this way. Only when the weather warmed up did Lilah's good mood return and Daisy realize how tense everything had been, for so long.

"I need to stop at home first," Lilah said when Wade turned onto Old Blackmun Road. "I need to change out of this dress."

Daisy felt a pinch of impatience. She wanted to get out of Wade's truck. She was thirsty and a little hungry. And she wanted to see Hugh Isherwood. Selfishly, she wanted to see what he would act like, now that the funeral was over. What would his face look like, in the house his mother would never enter again? Would he cry more or pretend to be jolly like Wade had in the truck? She wanted to see for herself, and quickly, before her mother showed up and prodded her to say hello to someone, to meet somebody else. She wanted to see, and then she wanted to go off in the woods, hide, go somewhere that she could think about these things without anyone looking at her, somewhere she didn't need to be concerned about the expression on her face.

So, when Wade pulled into the end of their drive and gently nudged Lilah on the arm, asking her where she got that bruise, Daisy hopped out of the cab and took off in a run.

"Hey!" he shouted, just as Lilah called her name. But she didn't look back. Winding around the big maple in the front of the house, its heavy widow-makers drooping as if they too were sapped by the heat, Daisy crossed into the woods toward the Ruin. This was what they had always called the shell of the house with its crumbling chimney, where they'd played every spring as soon as the ground was dry. Violet and Carna gave them old blankets and towels—scraps from Grandma Whitsun's old quilt shop—and all these would be hung up on sticks and weighted down by rocks to make curtains and forts and awnings and separate rooms. They were often joined by other kids who lived along Old Blackmun Road, morning games that would turn into runs in the sprinkler and swimming in the Isherwoods' duck pond, ending in barefoot dinners of grilled hot dogs while Violet and Evie Isherwood clustered around the patio drinking wine. That type of play pleased both mothers, though Mrs. Isherwood had always been adamant about her boys playing outdoors so as to keep her house clean, while Violet valued her girls having the sun on their backs and their feet in the dirt.

Of the three Whitsun girls, the habit had stuck only with Daisy. Once Poppy and Lilah outgrew playing in the Ruin and get-ting dunked by Wade and the Isherwood brothers, Daisy had been left on her own to rummage through the woods looking for mush-rooms or shotgun brass from deer hunters, to follow animal tracks and scat, her imagination unsatisfied by housebound pleasures. The boys on Old Blackmun Road still were outside, but they now had BMX bikes and BB guns, then four-wheelers and shotguns, all of which Violet quietly sniffed at. Violet wanted the natural ideal, nothing more artificial in her version of Eden than the wooden gate around her vegetable garden.

Daisy had no low opinion about four-wheelers or guns. She only saw the Isherwood brothers and Wade Dunedin ripping around in the dirt, screaming and yelling, having fun. Even Wade's religious cousins, the Haytches, who lived on the next farm over and passed their Sundays and Wednesday nights in an industrial chicken barn that had been turned into an evangelical church and posted up pro-life billboards on the edge of their property, had that kind of fun.

The older Whitsun girls had aged into dullness for Daisy. Poppy had no time for any of these retrograde country activities. She focused on her friends and her clothes, her sewing machine where she would experiment with things she'd found in the lost and found at Violet's Unitarian church, adding ruffles, ripping out hems, pleating and embellishing and gathering. And Lilah recused herself from that kind of fun, claiming a delicacy that seemed to descend along with puberty. She preferred to knit scarves that went on too long, with too many colors, or read endlessly on the sofa, her fingers sorting through her strands of white-blond hair while she turned the pages.

Daisy stayed in the woods. She would watch the boys in the same way she'd track animal prints and try not to feel so cheated. She was sure that had Lilah and Poppy wanted to hang out, the boys would have welcomed them. But without her sister and cousin, Daisy was locked out of the boys and their possibilities.

Perhaps this was why she was fascinated with Hugh Isherwood. The same age as Poppy, he'd been a mighty senior when Daisy was a meek eighth grader. In the school hallways, he was the good-looking athlete, always up for a prank or a party, surrounded by pretty girls. When she'd worked at his mother's strawberry patch, he'd been patient and kind, going out of his way to explain how to write out invoices and weigh the berry pails, giving her and the other kids rides on his four-wheeler from the barn to the fields. Twice he gave her a cold bottle of Gatorade, which she appreciated though she didn't like Gatorade. She knew at that time it wasn't politeness that made him do this; he and Poppy had dated briefly that spring, until Good Friday, when he'd gotten drunk and sent her a dick pic. Poppy, though no stranger to male attention, broke up with him immediately; she had a fussy side neither her mother nor her aunt could have predicted when it came to sex stuff. Poppy was fine with being admired, but the minute a boy got graphic about her body or his own, she was disgusted and over it. Whether this was due to the crudeness her midwife mother offered, with her talk of bloody breast milk and torn cunts, or her aunt Violet's preference for sugarcoated euphemisms ("apple blossoms" instead of nipples) was difficult to determine.

Even with Wade's truck long out of sight, Daisy kept running, dodging a series of gopher mounds. She made a shortcut across Old Blackmun Road toward the shelterbelt bordering the Isherwood farm, sweating as she passed over the coarse, dry grass and wilting wildflowers. Looping around a side yard full of parked cars and trucks, her sandals snapping over the sharp gravel of the driveway, she saw the Isherwoods' front porch, where circles of people gathered, talking and drinking. Enamel milk buckets full of geraniums, glossy-red rocking chairs set apart by an empty wire-spool table, ferns dribbling from pots hanging from the eaves. No Hugh, though.

She hesitated, though the screen door was open wide. Talking to adults was not her strong suit, and she was nervous around Hugh's father. Finally, she made herself push through the door.

Huddles of guests in Evie Isherwood's pretty living room murmured over plates. Women's voices, low and constant, streamed from the kitchen, followed by platters of vegetables and dip, crackers and cheese, Crock-Pots of barbecue meatballs, boxes of wine, bottles of whiskey and vodka. Everything a funeral goer could want to eat or drink. But no Hugh.

Daisy stepped through the sliding-glass door off the kitchen to the deck, where more people stood around the flower boxes of begonias spilling along the railings, then down the stairs to the patio, where Mr. Isherwood, his collar open and his tie off, sat next to his older son, Brian, along with Wade's dad and some other men she didn't know. Mr. Isherwood looked straight at her but didn't say hello. The men around him talked softly, and when one turned toward her, as if to ask her something, she panicked and rushed away, her dress swirling up as she bolted down toward the barn and the duck pond, feeling their possible stares on the backs of her thighs. Poppy's updo made her temples ache. As she ran through the Isherwoods' waxy, well-watered grass, she unpinned the clip Poppy had speared to her scalp, letting her hair lick the sweat of her neck and shoulders.

This time of day, tracking prints was impossible. The sun glared on the bright white gravel, no shading, no subtle gradations, no scrapes or mussing of the brush to follow. She ran past the wildflower garden Mrs. Isherwood had planted after an old tractor rusted and killed all the grass; a riotous stripe of pink coneflowers, black-eyed Susans, blue hyssop, scarlet beebalm, milkweed, and purple foxglove. She hid behind the willow tree that once had a tire swing they'd fought over when they were younger. Now there was a red bench bookended with tire planters full of impatiens. She paused to sit, and then heard voices and splashing coming from the duck pond. Of course! She jumped up, surged toward the water, stopping when she saw cast-off jeans and suit coats, a bare leg scissoring through spokes of cattails. She doubled back toward the barn and whipped inside, scurrying up the hayloft ladder as if she was being chased. Once up in the loft, she squinted and stepped carefully, her eyes adjusting to the shade. The floor beneath her sandals squeaked as she shrugged through cobwebs toward the hayloft door, where she scanned the pond until she found Hugh, treading water in a circle, his shoulders tan and wide, his hair the color of corn.

Two other boys she'd never seen before swam with him; one with long dark hair, the other a scrawny redhead. She guessed they were Ganey cousins from Evie's side of the family.

She tucked her skirt beneath her and sat down, keeping herself out of view. She remembered secreting herself up here when they were little kids; it was the place everyone wanted to claim first during a game of hide-and-seek. If you were fast enough, you pulled up the ladder behind you so nobody else could get to it. That was usually Hugh's and Poppy's move, because it took two to haul it up back then. Hugh, though not as mammoth as Wade, could probably haul anything he wanted now. And anyone. Except for Poppy.

She watched them swim. The splashing subsided, and they merely treaded water, squirted little streams through clenched palms, a trick Poppy had always tried to teach her but Daisy had never mastered. Poppy, who was not here, but still stuck in Daisy's mind. Poppy and her perfect style and perfect grades. Poppy a National Honor Society member and an All-Conference swimmer.

Poppy, who could sew a skirt in half an hour with two yards of fabric, and walk out the door in it, looking smashingly chic. Poppy, the Whitsun girl who could do everything.

Daisy had listened to adults ooh and aah over Poppy's abilities her whole life. But there was only one thing Poppy did that impressed Daisy: her mastery of the DivaCup. When she got her period, she had bragged to them how she could put it in and take it out without spilling a drop, and Daisy and Lilah had watched as Poppy made the little rubber cup disappear inside her body as she squatted in the bathroom they all shared. An hour later, Poppy reversed this magic trick, pulling the cup out and dramatically splashing it into the toilet bowl. This, more than school awards and official certificates tacked on a bulletin board in their attic bedroom, mesmerized Daisy, because even Carna said the DivaCup was a trick she couldn't manage unless she wanted to make the bathroom look like a slaughterhouse.

"I'd rather go through the hassle of a monthly extraction like in the old days than that goddamn DivaCup," Carna said. "While vacuuming out your innards is not for the faint of heart, I still maintain that maneuvering that cup is a bigger pain in the ass."

Lilah and Violet sewed their own flannel pads, not liking the waste and cost of menstrual products. Frustratingly, Daisy's period had not come yet, so she couldn't attempt this lone stunt of her cousin that she admired. Daisy liked to think she would be able to do it; she had always been more focused than Lilah, which was why Poppy preferred to teach her things. Poppy taught Daisy to read, to make oatmeal and grilled cheese sandwiches, to fold paper cranes for a mobile they'd given Violet for a birthday gift, to clip wet sheets to the laundry line so the wind billowed them like sails. And Poppy taught her to swim in this very duck pond; she held Daisy's small belly under her palm while all the other kids urged her to paddle over to them. All the mothers had been off to the side—their hands like visors over their eyes, chatting, looking at the flowers, drinking Diet Cokes in big plastic tumblers—Mrs. Dunedin still smiling and years from divorcing Wade's dad, Violet in her homemade sundress and muck boots, Evie Isherwood, tall and thin and alive, the diamond rings flickering in the sun as she gripped her drink. Even Carna, always so busy those days with her nursing boards, had been there when Daisy learned to dog paddle. Everyone cheered for her, and thinking of this, when the sun went behind a big continent of clouds, Daisy at last began to cry.

She had never been much of a crier. Even as a baby, Violet always marveled at Daisy's silence, her eyes on everyone, watching and smiling. She hadn't cried when she heard about Evie Isherwood's accident, nor when the details came out about a body so destroyed that the sheriff had to identify her by the cards in her wallet, the jewelry on her fingers. She hadn't cried when the family took her off life support, nor at the funeral, when Brian Isherwood read the lyrics of a song his mother used to sing him and Hugh at bedtime.

But the memory of the swimming lesson, how good and happy it was, that did it. She had to hold in sobs, so not to give away her hiding place. She tried to breathe, calm herself. The redhead boy floated on his back, his pale skin white against the greenish water.

Hugh was talking to the dark-haired boy in a regular voice that didn't carry. She swallowed tears, wished she could hear what he was saying. Was he talking about his mother? Even if he wasn't talking about her, he had to be thinking about her.

Though she had come from a farming family, Evie Isherwood had never quite fit the type. She never acted weary with too much work like Carna did, nor was she grubby from too much practicality, as Violet tended to be; she was not an earth-mama type like both Whitsun women, who lacked the vanity and the cash to do anything but let their blond hair darken. Mrs. Isherwood's hair gleamed a sunny blond; she always looked ready to be photographed, even when she was at the grocery store or weighing out berries for her pick-your-own customers. She liked tight, dramatic dresses with cinched waists and high heels, and she always sparkled with jewelry. Even one night when she saw her in her bathrobe, Daisy remembered Evie Isherwood wearing all of her jewelry. Diamonds from her husband, thin gold chains around her tan neck, one of those bracelets with the little individualized charms: a football for Hugh; a hockey stick for Brian; a pink breast-cancer ribbon for her sister who was in remission; a glittery red berry when she opened the pick-your-own patch.

How could he stand it, when everywhere you looked, there was something beautiful Hugh's mother had made or done. Maybe that was why he was swimming naked in a duck pond right now. Daisy had always lived around women and girls, and in her life, people were always talking, all the time, about everything: feelings, memories, aches and pains, wins and losses, gripes and grudges.

But she didn't know how boys and men went through their lives when it came to their words; they were either mysterious or hostile or silent, their tracks unclear, crossed over, littered with distracting debris. Difficult to discern.

A streak of reddish brown leapt across the white gravel, barking a solid bass line: Rusty, the Isherwoods' ancient Irish setter. Hugh called for him, and after some doubling back, Rusty jumped as he'd been taught from the dock into the water, all four legs boxed out into the air, the boys shouting approval. They shouted again when the dog's skinny skull split the surface and started bobbing as he paddled among them. Daisy sat up straighter, wiped more tears. She had always wanted a dog, and she had always loved watching Rusty swim.

But the dog's appearance signaled the end. The dark-haired boy hauled himself out, extending a hand to the redheaded one. Hugh ducked underwater and emerged a minute later, forearms on the dock, hollering toward Rusty, who swam through the cattails, disturbing a family of ducks, which squabbled and flew off over the thick green of the soybean fields. Hugh laughed, watching Rusty shake his dirty, wet fur next to the other boys.

Privately, she'd always thought Rusty was pretty homely. Snarly fur from life outside, livid sores on his forelegs that he constantly scratched and chewed. But she would have even taken an ugly dog. All of them had begged Carna and Violet for one, but their mothers were firm. She watched Rusty canter away; she would have petted him if he'd come to her all wet. Even if he was homely.

But Hugh, coming into full view, was anything but homely.

He had always been good-looking; but now he was even more so. The way he stood, comfortable in his bare self, the lower half of him hidden behind the wheelbarrow Mrs. Isherwood had up-turned and filled with petunias and some other tall blue bloom Daisy couldn't make out. Bachelor buttons? She watched as he took the T-shirt hanging off the wheelbarrow handle and wrung it out. The two other boys dried off with a red towel that looked way too plush for outside use; they'd probably nicked it from the master bathroom. She watched as they shook out their hair like Rusty, further blocking her view of Hugh, tossing the towel back and forth as they redressed in their funeral clothes. Finally, Hugh swiped it from between them and wrapped it around his waist, and there was a shout from the patio: Wade, Lilah, and a few other girls from school, waving in their direction. Lilah changed into her orange dress with the lemon-colored hem; it had always been too big for her, despite Poppy offering to take it in. One of the girls called out to Hugh to come over and Daisy figured he would. But he shook his head and waved them off, and Wade motioned them all to go toward the side yard, where they disappeared. It was un-nerving for Daisy to imagine having that power. In a towel, in a school hallway, at his mother's funeral party: what he agreed to was what happened. Stunned, she watched him gather his clothes over his forearm. Then he dropped his towel.

Well. Here was one part of him that couldn't be called good-looking. Not that it was ugly. Not quite. Mainly, it was strange and unlikely. The rest of Hugh's body was basic, well-known: his ruddy face, his wide shoulders, his knobs of biceps. Less familiar: his pale

stomach with a line of dark hair that trailed down to the prob-
lematic part. Which wasn't really a *part*, either. It was more a re-
gion, covered in hair darker than his head, the skin a different color
than the rest of him, which was standard white-boy farmer-tan.

He ducked into his T-shirt and pulled on his jeans. No underwear.

Could boys really do that? She cringed. She hated getting
dressed after swim practice, when her skin was even a little damp,
never mind dripping wet. Jeans, with the seams scraping between
her legs, were particularly awful. Maybe it was easier for guys; they
had no opening to rub against the stitching.

Carrying his boots, he walked barefoot to the bench under
the willow, hopping over the gravel drive—a relief to Daisy, as her
driveway had the same sharp pebbled rock—and sitting down, he
pulled a tin of snuff from his jeans and stuffed a wad in his mouth.
She hadn't known Hugh Isherwood chewed; she guessed it was a
recent habit. Poppy hated tobacco use of any type.

She watched as he put on his boots, the V of hair on his neck
dripping and darkening the back of his shirt. Every so often, he
leaned over and spat in the dirt. Then, laced up, he just sat there,
his arm spread over the back of the bench.

Nobody just *sat there* anymore, Daisy thought. They always
had to be doing something, and that something was usually looking at their phones. Because their mothers disapproved of screens
(Carna because of the cost, Violet, the lack of real-world connec-
tion), the Whitsun girls had been trained to keep their hands busy
with other things since they were young. Violet led by example; she
was always busy weeding her garden and reading her books, her

hands always tugging on a loop of hair while she watered or read or cooked. Carna and her cigarettes were less admirable, but she also had the finicky habit of stooping to pick weeds wherever she found herself having a smoke: the broken concrete outside her clinic, the cracked steps of her sister's church.

Even during the funeral, Daisy had seen people sneak looks at their phones, pick their fingernails, scratch their dandruff, unwrap sticks of gum, pick invisible bits of lint from their dress clothes. Never mind they were at a funeral, a death ritual, a spectacle involving a huge portrait of a dead woman in front of the heavy chocolate-colored cross with its matching pulpit and a rainbow of stained glass blooming colors from the sun outside, all backdropped with heavy, sad songs played by a giant organ that made the floors and pews vibrate. All of these things designed to captivate, but in the heart of the sanctuary, the audience still fidgeted and twitched with boredom.

Because she had still been inside her mother's body, Daisy had no memory of her own father's funeral. Lilah had been two years old and vaguely recalled being in a rowboat. Daisy considered this another instance of being cheated by her sisters. Poppy remembered some things, as she and Carna had flown to California to help with the arrangements and the move: there had been some singing and a guitar, then a boat ride to spread ashes in the ocean near Big Sur. Her father's mother had come, but she hadn't been happy about the ashes; she wanted her son buried where she lived in Myrtle Beach. But Violet said that her husband had never liked it there; he'd considered California his true home. On the rare occasions they visited her paternal grandmother—there had never been a grandfather in the picture, not even when her father was a kid—there was nothing of him to remember except pictures of him that she wasn't in. Though Daisy didn't like her grandmother in Myrtle Beach much, she thought she had a point; there wasn't a place to visit her father. He was a secondhand memory drifting through the Pacific, tiny ashy plankton riding the tides.

Up in the hayloft, staring at Hugh, at the fields with their still-scrawny sprouts, Daisy was undone again with sorrow. What good was it, for Evie Isherwood to watch her sons swim and play sports, to make sure the farmhouse on the land her family had owned for decades looked proper and presentable, repainting this barn, which had been put on a historic registry a few years back, opening a strawberry patch that everyone loved, if all that would happen is you'd be scattered over the dirt and probably blown away to North Dakota by summer's end? Miles from here, in every direction. Untraceable. Mixing with rainstorms and clouds and dirt from other people's crops, maybe ending up in the Atlantic, which Daisy had only seen the few times she visited Myrtle Beach, or perhaps the Pacific, which she had never been to, where microscopic bits of her father once floated amid kelp and sharks and plastic bottles nobody recycled. Had Mrs. Isherwood ever seen the ocean?

Daisy wiped her eyes again. It was stupid to be crying. It wasn't her mom who was gone. It wasn't even anyone in her *family*. If Poppy knew what she was doing, she might have smacked her. It was disloyal to even sympathize with Hugh Isherwood. Even from a distance. Poppy could always scent such disloyalty; and when she did, she would roust Lilah from the house, march to this hayloft, and yank Daisy down the ladder. There would be yelling, and Carna would shout to keep down the racket and Violet would arrive and attend to everyone's story and grievance, nodding and comforting until all the girls became annoyed with her, too. Her family was exhausting sometimes.

She lay on her side. Hugh hadn't moved. The sun had to be in his eyes because it was in hers, but he didn't seem to mind. He was either looking at nothing or looking at everything. At the blue sky, heavy over the black-and-green fields, or at the scatter of people around his house, coiling around trees and picnic tables. Could he see his mother's strawberry fields like she could?

The wood beneath her smelled clean and pure, different from the wood in the forest with its fans of fungus that lined the ridges of rotting bark. Violet had said once that the drier the wood, the less likely it was to harbor anything special; this was why people put pitch and shingles on their roof. The wood in the Isherwood barn had been baking under the sun for weeks, keeping fungi from exploding into life, slowing the tiny insects eager to make homes of rotting boards. Nobody had hayed horses in this barn for at least a hundred years, and it only stored tools and an old car without an engine, but Daisy knew that both Brian and Hugh had to clean it every season, raking nests from corners and sweeping dead leaves, caulking the cracks to seal out snow in order to preserve the structure as a relic. People have to work hard, Violet said, ripping creepers from her garden gate, to keep the forest from swallowing up what they'd built.

Daisy was surprisingly comfortable here, and yawned, thinking of the dream that had visited her the last few nights. It probably meant nothing, but it frightened her, and now, the sun warming her, she could feel all the sleep she had lost from it. She would lie here and look at nothing and everything, alongside Hugh, until the funeral ended and it was time to go home. How did you know when a funeral ended? Especially if you didn't bury the body in the ground that same day?

Maybe she slept. Maybe she dreamed she was back at home, nestled beside her sisters in their shared attic bedroom. Or maybe she dreamed she was still in the hayloft, that Hugh was still below her. Maybe she imagined the forest rushing in, insects and weeds and mushrooms devouring the barn's history, shredding it to the same timber confetti that was piling inside the dead maple in front of her house.

Wherever her mind went as her body lay still, she was interrupted by the sound of the ladder knocking against wood. Then the squeak of someone stepping on the rungs. She sat up, brushing her dress, shaking out her hair. One broad palm appeared on the wood floor, then another, with a brown bottle of beer. Then a face. Hugh Isherwood.

"You up here all alone?"

She got to her feet, nodded, wobbled in her sandals. They were actually Poppy's old sandals, not real leather. Her feet sweated. Hugh stood and finished the last sip of his beer.

"People are gonna come looking for you," he said. She hung her head in guilt. He meant Poppy of course. Maybe he'd been hoping she was Poppy this whole time. She felt a little pity for his single-mindedness. That Easter night, they had all lain in their beds, listening to Poppy explain how Hugh Isherwood was the person she'd miss the least when she left Hogestyn: "Bad enough he thinks I'd want a picture of his dick. I mean, even imagining a guy getting in position to take that kind of photo is just the worst. But that is *not* the world I'm going to live in, where the best thing a guy thinks he can give you is his stupid boner? Sorry, I don't care if you're drunk. You're still gross and stupid. When I get drunk, I don't act like that."

"When do you ever get drunk?" Lilah had murmured, but Poppy ignored this.

"Also, he has the worst name! I can't stand it. You never realize how much you have to say someone's name when they're your boy-friend. His name is so . . . nothing. It's like exhaling." She demon-strated: "Hhhhoooooooooooooooooooyoooouuuuuuu . . ." and they all laughed.

The laugh is what Poppy had been going for; her gift to them was to explain precisely what was terrible about any given thing—eyeliner pencils, their high school, pineapple on pizza, the shameful greed and poor design of fast fashion. That day had been awful—Hugh showing up during the Easter egg hunt at Violet's church, demanding to talk to Poppy, who screamed she was going to call the police while the little kids and their parents gawked, holding their candy baskets; Violet coming out to smooth things over, walking Hugh to his truck; Carna skipping dinner that night and claiming a migraine—they all wanted nothing more than to laugh it all off.

Later, in bed, Daisy had lain in the dark listening to the softening of her sisters' breathing and considered all their names. Her own: slippery at the beginning, soft at its end. Lilah: elongated, evaporating like Hugh's into the air. Poppy's a vexatious snap that made your jaw work.

"What were you doing up here?" Hugh asked. "Hiding?" His clothes were still damp and he was sweating pit rings. His hair slightly curled around his ears. He set the empty beer bottle behind a rafter.

"No," she said. She worried he was angry with her, that maybe he'd hoped to find his own solitude up here. She turned toward his house, looking for some explanation or excuse. The trail of Lilah's orange dress, the shout of Poppy's wrath. Only a group of men were out in the yard now, tipping their own beer bottles up in the sunshine.

When she turned back, Hugh was right next to her. Two inches away. She stilled, and he came closer. One inch away. He smelled like menthol snuff and pine needles and wet dirt. And beer, too. His blue eyes were watery and red, irritated by the pond water. His hand slid out of his pocket and onto her shoulder. He rubbed her neck and the material of her dress, then the side of her bare arm. He didn't seem mad. Maybe he would push her away.

But then he leaned down and pressed his mouth on hers. The smoothness of his lips, the sharp poke of stubble on his chin and cheeks. She wanted to tell him he had made a mistake.

He backed away. All her words died. His eyes were open, but

they didn't seem to be looking at her. A crow cawed, and out of the corner of her eye, she swore she saw it streak black past the hayloft door.

He kissed her again. This time, she was very aware of how their noses were touching. It had never occurred to her, the now-inescapable fact that noses would be involved in kissing. The word that kept tumbling through her mind was *polite*. It was polite, Hugh kissing her. Gentle and kind. Sweet.

Then his mouth opened and so did hers. And though still good, this was not polite and sweet anymore. Bumpy tongues, beer mixed with chew, the ghost of toothpaste she'd used this morning, the whiskers on his chin and cheeks. His hands slid up her body, his thumb tripping over where her dress zipped up the side. His palm wrapped around her back.

This had to be a mistake. Hugh Isherwood was big and important. He had better things to do than this. He was a boy that girls like Poppy were meant for, and he was a man, too (like Poppy, he was nineteen), and he drove tractors and trucks and ATVs and a motocross bike he bought from his cousin's shop in Hogestyn, and every year once football was done, he worked on his family's farm and his Ganey relatives' farms and he was loud and nice and never seemed too studious but didn't flunk anything, either. Why was he holding her so tight?

She pressed her hands against his chest, against the clammy T-shirt cotton, a place she had not ever imagined touching. She knew she should feel good, but she felt mostly sad. She wasn't sure if she was doing this with him, or if it was just something happening to her. Like the way Rusty might plod along sniffing a trail only to see a bird and bolt after it. One thing happening, and then another, and another, and another. One moment she sat through a funeral where every hymn seemed heavier and longer than the previous one, the next she was sweaty in the Isherwoods' barn, the next she was being kissed while feeling Hugh Isherwood's heart thud under her palm.

He rubbed his face in her neck. This can't be a mistake, she thought, and his hands slid around her waist, went up over her breasts. Another thing happening, slow and sure, like the time-lapse videos they watched in Science 9: here a glacier was receding or a coral reef bleaching, the oceans were warming, beaching whales and exciting jellyfish, while pollution changed the colors of leaves and the insects that hid on them, and look, moths were just a kind of sad butterfly, born of night cocoons to journey toward the light. She moved her own hands around his shoulders to draw closer to him and she could hear their breathing, out of sync, his coming through his mouth, hers a slight squeak whistling through her nose.

Hugh's hands by turns crushed her breasts and smoothed over them. There wasn't a lot beyond what her bra propped up, but he seemed to find it worthwhile. She ringed her hands around his waist, stopping around the belt loops of his jeans. She kept kissing him. Was there something he wanted her to do to him?

But that question got lost. One hand slid down to her hip, beneath her dress, soundlessly, so easy. She could feel his fingers gathering up the hem. A slight movement of her leg and she caught his hand between the fabric and her thigh. He breathed in deeply. She closed her eyes. It was a matter of lifting, his hand smoothing over her underwear, his fingers sneaking beneath the elastic. She gulped as he brushed through her pubic hair— "maiden hair" as Violet tried to get them to call it, instead of the more greasy-sounding "pubes" that Carna complained about women shaving these days. The Reverend Whitsun wanted her daughters so badly to find everything about their bodies, and indeed, the whole of creation, beautiful and poetic, a failed mission she never gave up.

Hugh's finger slid inside her.

Unease surged in her stomach. She stood straight, looked over his shoulder. Her underwear was still on. Was he breaking her hymen? Carna said hymens were a sexist construct; Lilah said you couldn't break something that naturally stretched; Poppy huffed with disapproval that her family was vulgar enough to discuss the topic at the dinner table. Daisy had only stared at her mother, who gave her a smile meant to quell any alarm. Age fifteen, the youngest Whitsun, she was always subject to hearing fierce opinions about things she hadn't yet experienced, especially on the issue of female biology.

"Do you like that?" Hugh said, his voice low.

She didn't know what to say, so she kissed him again. Inside her body, she ached and almost told him to stop. But then it felt sort of good. She knew she was slippery on his hands; she wondered whether that mattered to him. He pulled back and this time put in two fingers. Was this normal? Had Poppy let him do this?

Her whole body lifted as he pushed high inside her, and she fought to keep her feet flat. She didn't want him to think he was hurting her. After a while of this, he pulled his fingers out.

"Are you a virgin, Daisy?" His fingers held close to her, soft and wet.

"Um . . ."

"It's okay," he said. His fingers slid back and forth. "I wouldn't. Don't worry."

She didn't say anything. She wasn't sure what she was supposed to be worried about him doing. He pulled his hand out of her underwear in a soft snap of elastic. His wet fingers paused on her lower belly, then came out from her dress. Her underwear was twisted and riding up but she didn't fix it. He kissed beneath her left eye.

"You're so pretty, Daisy."

She looked down, unable to think of an answer. His mouth brushed into her hair beside her temple.

"I think it's cool how you don't look like your sisters."

She shrugged. Though it was sweet how he saw them as sisters; that was how she saw them, too. Even if she was the one Whitsun with dark hair. The one who looked most like her father.

He cleared his throat like he didn't know what to say. She had no idea herself. The wild thought of jumping through the hayloft door and running into the woods occurred to her. But then she saw he was looking down at his hands, the ones that had touched her, been inside her. Embarrassed, she turned away to look out toward the duck pond, which shimmered in the late-afternoon heat. An

ATV shrieked in the distance; the men drinking beer were now all in their shirtsleeves. She focused on the strawberry patch sign, which looked slightly crooked from this angle.

"Hey." He tapped her shoulder.

"Yeah?" She still focused on the sign, the brightly painted letters in a juicy round font with berries dancing underneath.

"I think . . . I don't mean to be weird or anything. But I think you're on your period."

She whirled around. He rubbed his thumb against his middle finger so she could see the shiny rust under his wide, short nails, a slick strand of blood lacing across his knuckles.

Chapter Two

The first time I bled was on the voyage across the Atlantic. Bess ripped rags into strips and told me where to pin them. Then she returned to huddling over our provisions, James's heavy waxed-canvas satchel containing all we owned kept tight across her chest. I was fifteen and Bess just twenty, and though some of the women made small chatter at nights when the winds were low, she was short with them. She would chide me for becoming familiar, even with the old ones.

"You must be watchful, Jane," Bess said. "Here, we are not amongst friends."

She did not have to say it. Our brother, James—only a year older than I—had been spooked at the docks and sold his passage for coin, which he pushed toward us with tears in his eyes. We were to cross unprotected and had scarcely passed over the gangway when I felt the eyes of the deckhands rake across me and my sister. Our necks were bare to these men who shared our tongue but spoke it slant. I did what my sister asked but chafed beneath her instruction. I did not take to the water, despite Bess's assurances that it was just a boat, like so many we'd grown up seeing our entire lives.

But a ship is not a boat. A boat is a plaything, a lark. Boats nestle close to their coasts, like ducklings to their mother.

Our mother had sheltered Bess and me, with stories and songs and sewing, our life of tiny stitches and scraps bought with our father's wages. Our father had been a carpenter; he had always said it was not for him, the sailor's lot, as his own father had not found luck on the water. As such, all I knew of fishermen and sailors was their drunken swaggering and singing once ashore. None of this prepared me for a voyage that was no breathless adventure. Rather life aboard ship was akin to being confined inside a heaving animal barely tamed by rough men who scrambled about, making sorcery with shouts and ropes. I hadn't considered that foul weather would be worse at sea. I hadn't considered that waiting while feeling the tumble in one's gut would be the main task of a passenger.

I never thought of us as creatures. I thought as Mother had: about the luck and safety within Noah's ark, the world rescued from sin by gopherwood and faith.

A true ship was nothing of the sort. It was a dank cave of groans, teeming and stewing in fever, kettles of filth the waves flung across our dark quarters. During stormy weather, I tried not to open my eyes. Hearing the din was all I could manage. In a ball beneath my traveling coat, many nights I breathed the thick air while Bess murmured into my ear: *This is the water, this is the water, beneath us is the same earth, the same one. Soon, soon we will arrive.*

But this is the water now, you must believe it, you must accept it just as your insides slosh within you, like a baby in a womb sloshes and makes a woman startle in sleep.

That first time, Bess fed me biscuits. She sheltered me with our quilt each night while I removed my soiled rags and then she folded me into sleep and took them away, to where I didn't know. Days of nausea passed, one tumbling into another, until one morning, I woke, and felt stillness within me. True calm. The waves were slight, gentle. The rags pinned between my legs were clear of blood.

I went above deck to see the sun and that was how the truce came with the water, at last. Myself and Bess and two other old women looked at the waves and the sun for so long I lost any sense of time. The sailors smiled and the winds were strong but the ship soared through them, smooth and swift. How I want to remember this day with nothing but the pleasure it was! Bess shared our bread with the old women, and one of the deckhands bowed to her as she walked past him. Later came the sunset, and all were entranced by the light melting over the horizon. One of the sailors turned one of the old women in a polite jig. The dancing woman and the red-faced sailor twirling in the calm of this view, only the creaking of sail and rope and water for music. A deckhand clapped along, his eyes crawling over me, then fixing on Bess.

I should have seen this for the ill omen it was. But I had our mother's devotion to pretty stories. Our mother saw meaning in all things, would have called the woman dancing as a signal to celebrate—Miriam dancing on the shore after her brother Moses parted the Red Sea. But after our father's death, our mother was lost to us in Roscommon, confined to the madness that plagued her family for generations. Her pretty stories a jumble of her many wild notions.

I never knew if Bess had seen what was to come.

I woke one morning to sounds of rain and wind, Bess's bruised face across from mine. Her shirtwaist torn beneath our quilt, her breath short as if it hurt to breathe.

"I have fallen," she said. "Pay it no mind. Stay below. We shall make landfall soon. Mr. Ganey's letters are in the satchel."

I brought her water, which she wouldn't drink. I wrapped her in the quilt. I waited and prayed. I slept, my mind brittle and unsettled. But I did not wake when she left my side that night to slip beneath the calm murk. I would not have believed it, until the old woman who had danced on the deck shook her head and gathered me toward her.

"Those beasts," the old woman said. "Is there nothing holy that they would not sunder? Do not speak, lass. It will only encourage them."

I later understood why Bess spoke of the letters. Inside the satchel, on an envelope sent long ago to her by Mr. Ganey, she had scratched her last words.

I am ruined, she wrote. *Many times over. I bear the fault of it, and I regret I am not strong enough to stand between you and what comes next. I love you, dear one.*

The second time I bled was my wedding night. Though I was not who Arthur Ganey had been promised, after consultations with his sibling, I was deemed acceptable by him and his sister,

Maude. My quietness did not bother Arthur; he was also a quiet sort. This time I pinned rags I'd found in the pantry, and that evening in the dark if Arthur realized his second-pick of a bride was bleeding, he must have thought it was virgins' blood; his slowness and timidity during the act itself suggested he worried over hurting me. After removing himself from my body, he filled the ewer with fresh water so I might wash and brought me a clean cloth from the kitchen. I repinned my rags and waited for what might come next. But Arthur was silent. He lay back down and slept. He did not return to our wedding bed for the rest of the summer.

Later, Maude Ganey would tell me he slept fitfully. That his mind troubled over the farm. He had been spoiled, she said, her voice shy and secret. Unaccustomed to sharing, the only son, she said; they'd had a brother who died before Maude came, and another babe that was born dead, taking their mother with it. This reasoning struck me as odd. Arthur never touched me again for any reason and continued to spend the small hours elsewhere. I never asked Maude why this was, though she entreated me to her confidence. We were to be as sisters, she said. But I had been sisters with Bess, and Maude could not compare. Maude was sterner and stricter than a sister should be. She insisted we stitch straight hems on pillowcases, no lace, no embellishments. We ate breakfast with china so delicate I was nervous to touch it. She never spoke of where to put my soiled rags. Once the bleeding ceased, I burnt them in secret in the firepit behind the kitchen one night. I watched them twist like living things and my mind hardened like tempered metal. I resolved to reach for my new husband.

My parents had not always lived pretty, but pretty stories be damned. Though I had no one to instruct me, I knew that being a good wife, despite my youth and inexperience, was essential. I had survived much on the voyage across; God's ferocious waters could not take me. I was all defiance and bravery.

Though they often shared it with their children, my parents always shared a bed. My father was not timid, but neither did he wander or take to drink, despite my mother's odd ravings. A marriage wasn't all sweetness, but there was companionship to be had, and I was intensely lonely. Thus I went out in the evening wrapped in my shawl to see if I could find Arthur. Perhaps, under the stars, far from the sharp ears of his sister, he would tell me his secrets. Perhaps this coaxing was the job of a wife of a quiet man.

I did not find my husband that night nor the next. I wavered in my resolve and felt shamed at not being a shiny enough lure, until I found the man who deigned to be caught.

Chapter Three

Daisy stepped into the shower, hitching up the door so it would close properly. Their house was full of compromises like this. Faucets dripped, windows didn't open, the stovetop needed a long match to ignite, the washing machine only worked on the heavy-duty setting. Though it had belonged to Evie Isherwood's family, no one had lived in it since the seventies. Rob Isherwood wasn't a bad landlord, but he had a way of letting little things pile up long enough that the Whitsuns had to find work-arounds.

She held her ruined underwear under the spray. There was blood, but also spangling down her fingers were bright swirls and blackish snarls, like severed bits of a living creature. Once the stains faded from scarlet to pink, she slapped the underwear over the glass door, and then got to work scrubbing herself, rubbing the bar of soap on her armpits, under her breasts, between her legs. Hugh had no idea this was her first period. She couldn't decide if that made things worse or better. He had been worried, inviting her to come inside, reassuring her that everything was okay, but Daisy realized that was probably because he thought she'd tell Poppy. She had climbed down the ladder and was halfway across the service road before he could even holler after her.

After she was clean, she wrapped in a towel and searched beneath the sink for pads. There was a box of tampons, but the thought of shoving her own fingers up there right now upset her. Pads seemed much less complex. She trailed across the house in her towel to the laundry nook, where she found some clean underwear in a basket and one of Poppy's bras—she and Poppy wore similar sizes. She pressed the pad into the crotch of her underwear and then quickly dressed. But the cutoff shorts she normally wore made her feel like she was smuggling something down there. She pawed through the heap of clothes for something less binding and, though they were too short, settled on a pair of pajama pants of Lilah's. Dressing out in the open felt reckless, but for once, nobody was home. She wasn't ashamed of her body, really; Carna was always very matter-of-fact about nudity, and Violet always said having no men under their roof. But none of the Whitsun girls besides Lilah were in the habit of going around naked or even half dressed.

Her stomach growling and churning, she went into the kitchen and ate some strawberries from the fridge. Then a banana, and a bowl of granola with almond milk—Lilah was on some anti-dairy kick lately—and some homemade trail mix that was stale. She imagined Hugh, sitting down to a plate of sandwiches and pasta salad and potato chips. She loved that kind of food. Picnic food, grill-out food, summer food. She found a bottle of ibuprofen in the cupboard and gulped down two tablets with two glasses of sweet tea. It was after seven o'clock and clouds were dimming the lowering sun. Her belly, now full, ached. She wanted to lie down but it would be stiflingly hot upstairs, even if she turned on the fans and opened the windows. She dragged the double-star quilt off the sofa and went to the back porch.

Carna sat most nights out here, drinking her whiskey and smoking cigarettes that she crushed out in a chipped white dish with an angel painted in the center of it. Her aunt had never explicitly claimed this space but for years it had always been where she alone sat in the quiet, drinking, smoking, not rejecting company but rarely inviting it. Her bedroom had a similar force field around it—Poppy was the only one who would enter it without asking—in contrast to Violet's bedroom, which was always open for morning cuddles or if someone had the flu, no permission necessary.

The back porch looked directly out onto Violet's garden and what had been Carna's chicken run. Raccoons had picked off the last of her hens two summers ago, and while everyone missed the eggs, nobody missed the birds. Carna said she had enough brooding mamas under her care.

The pain in Daisy's belly rippled, moving up toward her breasts, and down to the tops of her thighs. She leaned back on Carna's lounger and let her bare feet stretch toward the late sun that slashed over the cushions. Her toenails were unvarnished squares and there was a slat of hair she'd missed shaving on her left ankle. She couldn't decide if she should get up and quick scrape it off with one of the razors in the shower; being the only dark-haired girl in the Whitsun house always made her self-conscious.

It was a luxury to be in the house alone. The woods and the ravine were the places she usually escaped to, trading the hectic crash of voices and bodies for the crunch of leaves and dead branches beneath her feet, the call of birds too far above her head to be seen. But Carna's back porch was also peaceful. The quilt soft on her smooth legs, the lounger's slope easing the pain in her belly. The air smelled like it might rain. Finally, Daisy did not pray, but for this she felt thankful, after so many days of thick, unceasing heat.

The sun lowered. Thunder groaned in the distance. She imagined the people at the Isherwoods', looking at the sky, evaluating whether to go in, take down the picnic table's umbrella, fold up the chairs. She imagined Hugh, done eating, staring out the window. Staring at everything and nothing from inside the home his mother had made and now would never enter again. Would he speak? Would he laugh? Would he tell those boys he'd swam with in the duck pond what he'd done? Would he send her a picture like he'd sent Poppy? He had her phone number, from her days at the berry patch. But she had left her phone upstairs by her bed, plugged in since the battery was shit. She tried to imagine him taking a picture like that again. For her, for Poppy, for anyone. But she could only see his watery eyes, his expression at that last minute where he looked unsure what to say or do next. She listened to the crickets, sighed. And the rain came: first, light spatters on the roof, then fine misting through the screens, nudging her into sleep.

◆

◆

◆

The dream was like the storm itself. At first timid, then stronger. Rattling the screens, flashing eerily as water splashed through the trees. The faceless woman with the red-gold hair sitting on an old hospital bed holding a small alabaster jar. Embedded in the jar's cork was a silver needle, which she held between her thumb and pointer finger. The needle winked and then disappeared as the woman rolled the coarse bed linens over her, hiding her body with the sheets or her nightgown; it wasn't clear where one began and the other ended. She pressed the needle into the fabric, her long hair fluttering with each jab. There was no blood; Daisy always expected blood when needles were involved. Learning to sew with Carna had involved sudden finger pricks that bloomed perfect globes of red. But the dream's unseen logic assured Daisy that the faceless woman was too skilled for such errors. This needle wasn't meant to puncture skin but inflict a message on the fabric. Mechanically, repetitively, the faceless woman poked the material with one hand, whisking it along like a scroll across her knees with the other.

Then, an empty white-tiled room, a fogged-up window providing the only light. Cold, wet sheets wrinkled over the woman's body in layers, her nipples pricking up as she shivered, her hair in slats across her face. Two nurses hauled her shaking body across the room and slipped her into a white porcelain tub with a splash. Daisy could feel the water in this part, a shocking icy temperature that made her panic as if it were her own body. An uncomfortable while later, the woman surfaced from the water, her limbs steaming, her hair like a pile of wet feathers, her mouth stretching wide into a pink bow.

But now, Hugh appeared. Shimmering, like a hologram; he was both there, and yet not. Daisy wanted to move and found herself trapped, immobile under the water, beneath the tight freezing sheets. The tiled room disappeared and night shot forward to morning. Streaming over Daisy's body were the beads of water, dotting the old worn wood of the hayloft. The sunlight turned away and became the heat of a banked chimney fire. The woman stood, no more sheets, and then lay beside Daisy, legs long and pale and opening at the knees. Water steamed and poured out from between them, but Daisy could feel it alongside her, the dilation of every pore, the wet slide in her panties just like the period blood, the surge in her stomach that almost hurt. She couldn't see Hugh but could feel the pressure and the lift of his fingers inside her. Daisy and the faceless woman lay next to each other, not the same person, but feeling the same things.

A man's voice, softer than the drops of water: *Take your hair down.*

A woman's laughter.

The man's voice: *Live in my heart and pay no rent.*

And then just breathing, each breath subtracting a small chunk of the panic from before. The weight of a body beside her, above her. Hugh. And then the woman, her face turned away, her hair brushing her elbow propping her up on the floor. The woman spoke, then. But Daisy could not understand the words. She could see the woman's mouth, slowly appearing amid the watery pool where her face should have been. Her lips were pale pink, furiously repeating, all the while her belly contracted. The pressure inside her, between her legs, between what could be felt and what could not be seen, continued to grow.

Daisy knew she shouldn't feel these things with this woman, but she couldn't stop any of it. The feelings inside her pushed and rushed. There was no end to it. It was painful and delightful. Embarrassing and exhilarating. She opened her mouth to say Hugh's name but she couldn't find words.

The woman fell back against the floor, her skull a crack of lightning.

Her scream shattered through Daisy's body: *Come back come back come back oh please come back to me.*

The woman turned to her, her nose now emerging above the chanting mouth, her own hand between her legs, her bare body trembling, her beautiful hair singed with sunlight. For a moment, the sun flashed and Daisy could almost see her. Almost. One more moment, and she would.

And then it was gone. The rain, the storm, the pressure, the ache in her stomach. There was nothing but the wet wooden floor of the back porch, the feeling of heaviness yanked away like a chain, and then the crash of the old maple tree and its widow-makers sweeping against the roof of the house, a great knocking like the hand of God announcing its presence.

Chapter Four

The water had tried to pull me down into it; I believed then, I caught between one man and another, that maybe only fire could take a girl like me. The winds rush across these trees and the sun rises and falls each dusk, and the water drenches the fields until they thicken with mud, and in winter, everything dies. In spring, girls and calves and foals are born and men stand over all of them to assess their worth, as they do everything else that is worked and pushed and turned until it wears out and cracks and decays. Everything, but me.

A few days beyond the waters that became my sister's grave, a storm arose as we approached the harbor. The ship pounded and cracked. Water pooled beneath our feet, soaking our cases, dousing the banked fire. The old woman protecting me began to pray, and the crew shouted for us to man boats. There was a crush to climb on deck, and once above, the shore was blurred with gray rain. The wind shoved us across the boards like crockery off a table. The old woman tried to hold on to me but she was not strong enough.

It was relief, the first moments, as the satchel dragged me lower and lower. The water greenish, then gray, then dark. Pure silence. It was the first quiet moment since leaving home.

That my body began to fight, to force its way up, happened under a power not my own. I rose like a plant seeking sun, the satchel winding around my neck. I was buoyant as if by some magic. Then hands, hard and certain as iron, gripped my shoulders, next my hips, and I was out from the water, and into the boat of a Finn named Jarvinen.

The hands were not the Finn's but belonged to a man who said he'd been as apt to pluck a diamond from the mire as a redheaded girl strangling on a heavy canvas bag. After he tipped me to the side and beat the water from my lungs, he stated his name, Patrick Casey. He pushed the hair from my eyes and asked if I knew James Murphy and his sisters, for he was to take them to his employer in a place called Minnesota.

I didn't answer him, and the Finn hauled us to shore; later I was given dry clothes and a bandage for a slash on my left arm, a wound that would heal just days before I married Arthur Ganey. In Jarvinen's boat, Patrick Casey had asked me if I knew what had cut me, and I had said it was the sea. The Finn told Patrick to look for wounds around on my head, which he did, finding not a scrape.

"Your fine hair," he would say, "Too fiery to let you sink. My mermaid girl. A gem too good for Neptune's chest."

I liked this tale. I still like it. It was prettier than the truth and did not gut me like Bess offering herself to some dreary ocean god. But I did not have a remembrance of any of it. Months later, when we lay together, hidden by night and stealth, his beard scraping against my bare belly, Patrick would tell me the first words I had spoken to him.

"My brother, James, would not come," I'd said. His satchel still wound around my dress, where Arthur Ganey's letters were nothing but wet pulp, heavy as a cross. "And my sister, Bess, is gone to rest in the ocean. I am Jane. I am the only one."

+
+
+

The land where Arthur and Maude Ganey lived was beautiful. I did not want to like it, but I did. Even when rain raged across the fields and the whole earth seemed to be darkening under a dome of clouds, I found it beautiful. Like a storm being held under a giant teacup. I wondered where my husband laid his head when the rains raged that summer. I would look out the back door of the kitchen toward where the chickens were kept to the fenced field where the new cattle my husband had purchased from his neighbor Paul Haedesch nipped at grass, to beyond that, the forest that kept its own secrets.

I was kept, too. Enclosed, surrounded, fed and watered at Maude Ganey's table. I was waiting for something to grow inside me that Arthur would not plant. My courses came: June, July, nothing in August, which gave me a start—how could our first (and only) coupling in the spring wait to manifest so long? But then came September's courses, ruining the petticoat that Bess had made for me before we'd left (it had a row of miniature green horses cantering around the waist). Arthur had never seen it. I burnt the soiled part and used the scrap of green horses to tie back my hair, until Maude told me she found that gaudy for the mistress of a house, that Arthur would not like it. I kept it tied to the inside of my chemise after that, another place Arthur would not see. For the tinker selling pots and saddles received more attention than Arthur showed me. He was as much of a husband as mist on a rainy morning, and his eyes like dark stitches beneath his heavy gold hair offered the same amount of warmth. He always looked past me, away from me, his shoulders sagging wearily. His voice only animated when he talked with the hired men or the Haedesch brothers who came in the evenings to talk of farming and prices for meat and milk while Maude and I sewed in silence.

Women came to visit, of course, as I was a new bride. But even then, I felt shy and my stitching became wild and untidy and much of it I later ripped out. The women's visits involved discussions of their gardens and fruit preserves, their children's illnesses, the packages of needles and buttons they sought, the rumors of a new church to be built, the names like thudding bricks—Haedesch, Gudrunson, Carlsburg—and the stories of other women I did not know, in particular a woman called Mistress Hellerstadt and her unending boasting about her singing lessons. Of these strangers, Mistress Hellerstadt was the least intriguing to me. The woman who lived alone by the river, who made crank tonics for fools who still believed in what they called "devil's witchery" was the one I wondered after. The nervous glances exchanged in Maude's parlor when they spoke of the river woman made me itch to know the scandal. But the women who visited did not elaborate; though a proper bride, perhaps I was too young to know such things. These women looked at me in pity; the only time they addressed me directly was to offer condolences for my sister. I did not know how much they knew of Bess's death—I certainly did not tell Maude or Arthur her fate but couldn't be sure of what I had said to Patrick Casey in Jarvinen's boat. Still, I suspected they only broached the topic because they were seeking out scandal just as I was of the river woman. I could not speak of Bess without the ocean that had swallowed her rushing up in my throat.

Still, these visits were the only moments where I might feel the slightest bit comforted, light talk chattering amidst the teacups and soft settling of sewing on laps. Maude was making room for me amongst the skirts and bits of history offered here; I could see my place being set amongst these stories of babies and musicales and lost cows in blizzards and quilts at church picnics. But I dreamt of escaping out the front door, toward the violence of the sea, running and screaming with laughter with my sister, our dogs at our heels, men in the lane shouting dirty jokes as we tumbled before the cliff's end.

✦
✦
✦

I turned sixteen that first Minnesota winter and slept alone each night of it. I hadn't grown up in a house as big as the Ganeys' farmstead, but our home was no mean thing. In it, we remained close in a way I never found in Maude and Arthur's walls. Nights back home I shared a bed with Bess, and my father and mother and my brother were always close by, as was the heavy brick hearth my grandfather had built. Every day was a churn of friendly talk, jokes about our neighbors, oaths and curses and songs. Before the fire took our home and Father, that is, and before my mother was sent away to her Roscommon kin. She never saw our father's grave. None of us would leave our mark for others to visit, as it was.

I don't like to contemplate that but I often do. Time is unkind even when it's the only thing you have.

The loneliness of young girls is eternal. I feel it always: the way it was and the way it is. My Whitsun girls stretch toward it like leaves to sun, set upon lessons and chores, unbound by dreams of their own kitchen and crockery, their own quilts and dresses and boots. Young women, loose in the woods, naked in the grass, laughing and shouting in a way that would have brought more than a scolding had I done it and been caught.

I marked an end of loneliness—a pause, in hindsight—that spring. I had abandoned hopes of Arthur loving me, of being a companion. I burnt my rags in the firepit behind the summer kitchen each month, their ashes deepening the creases of Maude Ganey's eyes. I came to feel that I had nothing, that I made nothing, and therefore there was nothing left to lose.

That spring was when I made my own fire. I rolled down my stockings, wrapped in my shawl, and walked through the ditch full of thistle and dandelions. Once out of sight, I would remove my boots and let my bare feet feel the cool, damp earth amongst the trees. Arthur did not love me; he did not look on me with tenderness and care. His face softened only at day's end, when he sneaked whiskey far from Maude's notice and sighed toward the sun setting over the Haedesch farm. Maude sighed similarly each morning across from me at the table. Bess was gone, James was gone. Inside me was the stark howl of a single wolf. I walked through trees, felt the brush scrape the skin that no one ever touched, heard the squeaks of creatures hidden all around me. I looked for those cliffs near the roaring sea, a silly girl's quest, but came to naught but more fields, or woods that might yet become them.

The serving girl became accustomed to my solitary walks, settling the flowers I picked into Maude's pretty vases; she told me where I might find berry patches and Queen Anne's lace. I sought out oaks for acorns, as James had once liked to carve them into buttons and playthings for us as children; and I gathered black walnuts, which stained my hands and my apron, causing Maude to frown and the serving girl to say she would give them to Patrick, who tended the stock. "He took the acorns, but said the walnuts are only suited for pigs," she explained later, grimly tipping them into her apron to cart home to the Haedesch farm.

"Are you well acquainted with our land yet, Jane?" Maude would ask when I would return, my hair spilling from its cap and my boots dusty. "Shall I assign you to make a map of each berry patch and rose bower?" This would make any visiting ladies titter and I would apologize for my unkempt state. But I would not give up wandering; there were endless nooks one could find to hide in throughout the Ganey farm, where none of my sister-in-law's frowns could reprove me, where I could think of Bess and James and Mother and Father without worrying about the expression on my face.

I avoided most of the settled parts of the farm that spring. I knew well the skeleton of the barn and outlines of the fields and the stables where Patrick Casey tended horses. I avoided the men working the Ganeys' land; I was young but old enough to understand that my sojourns might look like flaunting.

But one day, after tumbling over the backs of fallen trees and watching a beehive swarm and split across the blue skies, I became turned around and found myself at the hut that adjoined the stable, long after dusk. The distant rustling of horses swept over me as I stared at Patrick Casey's untended fire. And then he appeared, from the woods, holding a clutch of sticks and a reel of dead rabbits. His eyes were wide at the mistress's visit.

"If you're looking for Arthur, you're off a few paces," he said, nodding west.

"I'm not looking for Arthur," I said.

He set down the sticks and his catch. The eyes of the rabbits were cloudy black.

"You're a rather young thing to be looking for anything else this time of night."

"Your fire was inviting," I said. "And you're not so old yourself as to be calling me a young thing."

He nodded, and then we did not speak. I watched the fire, I watched him whet his knife and then clean his catch. I wrapped the shawl around me, I heard an owl call to another above us in the trees. At last, he finished his tasks.

"You keep late hours," I said.

"You as well, ma'am. Why is that, a man could wonder."

"I haven't an answer for you. What keeps you awake?"

"I've been building," he said. "Not enough time for what needs attention."

"The fields will soon need that."

"Aye, but I am not a hand for that, missus. I tend to the stock, the horses. Ganey hasn't a knack for either."

"Is that so?" I asked. "I know little of him."

"There's little you'd want to learn, young missus. Pardon me, will you? Won't be but a minute." He stepped inside the hut, the wood door sticking like it hadn't been properly shimmed. Moments later he came out with a bottle and a tin cup.

"You'll have a taste; it'll help you rest," he said.

His eyes went over my body when he handed me the tin cup. I stood and sniffed and drank it down. Whiskey, with a bit of rust. My father had warned me that my mother's people could not tolerate strong drink, and I had only sipped it once while feverish. I coughed and wiped my mouth, and he smiled.

"You came on an ill night, in any event," he said. "Rain is coming."

I remember looking for whatever sign he saw. The night around us was thick; I had watched the sunset and not seen any indication of poor weather. I might have explained—this place wasn't by the sea, so the water offered no help. Instead, I put my eyes to his, and the dark around me felt less potent.

"Shall I return when the weather is fairer?"

"Call on me whenever you like, young missus," he said.

Chapter Five

When Daisy surfaced, Poppy was on the pool deck, her legs lean and wet, her mirrored goggles tucked into the hip of her swimsuit, dangling like a pair of silver eyeballs. Daisy took off her own goggles and started to climb out, but Poppy held out a hand.

"Wait," Poppy told her, goggles bouncing against her thigh.

Daisy hung on to the concrete lip of the pool. Lap swim was ending soon. Perry Coughlin was lifeguarding today, pulling the lane markers out of the water so that the water aerobics class could start. Daisy could see the old women in their skirted suits and plastic flip-flops gathering near the deep end, watching him. The tampon inside her was like a sharp plastic cork. It had bitten into her every lap she'd swam. The morning had been insanity. Violet and Carna circled the yard as they inspected the damage: the roof was wrinkled and mussed, as though the old maple had been a giant splayed hand trying to whisk it off like a dirty bedspread. The whole scene disgusted Poppy, as if a tree felled by a storm had been another poor choice on the part of her mother and aunt. Feeling unsettled by the strange dream and the force of the storm, when Poppy said she was going to swim some laps, Daisy asked to come along.

Daisy put her goggles around her wrist like a bracelet and floated her legs behind her. Her cap was rucking up, pulling her hair and giving her a headache. She couldn't see who Poppy was talking to, because the water aerobics ladies were now huddled by the ladder for their class, but whoever it was wore street clothes. And was a guy. Of course Poppy would just stand there, perfect and dripping wet, talking to a guy like it was natural; she had done the same thing when they arrived, chatting with Perry, her body proud as a morning glory opening in the sun, while Daisy stood with her arms crossed over herself, despairing of how her toenail polish had rubbed off and looked trashy. Daisy had been friends with Perry's younger sister, Gretel, since sixth grade and going to their huge house on the west side of Hogestyn always meant hoping to sneak a few looks at Perry as he did homework under the chandelier at their dining room table or played video games on the enormous TV in their luxurious finished basement. Gretel had been on vacation with her cousins in Colorado most of June. She wasn't due home until August and she was terrible at keeping in touch, sending dumb texts and funny pictures of dogs skateboarding or kids wiping out on trampolines instead of any real information. Though she missed Gretel, Daisy couldn't figure out a way to announce *Guess what, I finally got my period* in that context.

Daisy pulled her cap from her ear to drain water; the tampon pinched again. The whole workout, she had imagined a red plume streaming behind her as she struggled behind Poppy through the various sets: two hundred freestyle, four fifty-meter breaststroke sprints, a series of IMs. She shifted and the pinching did, too. The morning sun splintered through the high windows of the pool, making jagged stripes on the red bleachers, and then the water aerobics ladies were in the water and she could finally see who her sister had been making her wait for: Wade Dunedin in his Day-Glo road-crew vest and work clothes. He looked sweaty and unhappy. Poppy was edging him toward the exit; Perry Coughlin was the kind of guy who would freak about someone wearing boots on the pool deck. Daisy pulled herself out of the water.

Wade was not budging. Just as the water aerobics music started up with a club mix of "It's Raining Men," Daisy approached.

"Jesus Christ," Wade was saying. "You think I'm some kind of fucking asshole? I was just looking out for her."

"What's going on?" Daisy asked. Across the pool next to the lifeguard chair, Perry stood with his hands on his hips and stared at them.

"Does she know, too?" Wade asked, nodding at Daisy.

"Know what?"

"Never mind," Poppy said, her eyes on Perry, and then Daisy. "Wade, we have to go."

"Will you talk to her, though?" Wade asked. "Just tell her . . ."

"Yes, for fuck's sake," Poppy said. "I already told you!"

He clutched Poppy's elbow. "I'm not trying to be a dick," he said. "I know she's had some stuff going on."

Poppy's eyes flamed up in the familiar way that always made Daisy flinch, and she recoiled, but Wade, oblivious to what that look meant, put his hand on her older sister's wrist and repeated his request. Daisy stopped breathing for a second. She watched her sister pause, too. Poppy had particular reactions to people touching her, telling her what to do.

"Poppy," Daisy started, unsure what to say.

"Hey, guys?" Perry Coughlin, walking toward them, his Adidas slides smacking the tiles.

"Hey, Perry," Poppy said. Her voice was annoyed, but she still smiled.

"Why don't you, you know? Maybe have your conversation out in the lobby?" Perry said, staring directly at Wade, whose face instantly bloomed red.

"Why don't you, you know, maybe go jack off a bobcat?" Wade said, letting go of Poppy.

"Hey!"

"Come on," Poppy said, pushing Wade toward the exit.

"Mind your business, dickhead," Wade said over his shoulder.

"We're leaving, Perry, I'm sorry," Poppy said. "Come on, Daisy."

"Tell her what I said," Wade called as he pushed his way out to the lobby, Perry standing back, whipping his whistle around his knuckles.

Poppy nodded, aggravated. "Daisy, would you move! Jesus Christ."

Her sister's hand on her, prodding her forward, Daisy rushed through the locker room door.

"Daisy, what the fuck . . ." She stopped, and Poppy pointed. There was a trickle of blood curling around the back of her thigh.

"Did you finally get your period?" Poppy asked.

"Shut up!" Daisy hissed, though the shower area was empty. Poppy laughed roughly, and Daisy darted into the bathroom stall. Poppy was right behind her, pushing the door open before she could latch it.

"Why didn't you say anything?"

"Nobody was really around."

"Are you wearing a tampon? Or just nothing?"

"A tampon," she said. "I'm not an idiot."

"Well, what size is it?"

"I don't know! Get out of here!"

"You idiot!" Poppy said. "Why didn't you say something?"

"It hurts enough," Daisy said. "I don't need to be yelled at!" She sat down on the toilet with a thud.

"It shouldn't hurt," Poppy whispered. "Maybe you didn't get it in far enough."

"I did, though. It's all the way in there."

Poppy put her hands on her hips. "Did you . . . Okay, take it out, will you? Let me see what it looks like."

"No!"

"I won't look at *you*, I just want to look at *it*," she said. "Come on. We gotta bring the car back for my mom."

Daisy waited until Poppy looked up and away, and then reached down between her thighs, her hand just an inch over the cold toilet water, her fingers pruney and soft, fishing out the tampon.

"Jesus!" Poppy said, a little loud. "No wonder it hurt!" She spun the toilet paper roll with a slap and then lowered her voice. "You didn't take out the applicator. You only use that part to help put it in," Poppy added.

"What do you do with it?" Daisy mumbled, her eyes opening to see the bloody mess flash from her sister's fist, wrapped in toilet paper, to the little silver tin bolted to the stall's wall.

"You just throw it away," Poppy said. "Some of them don't come with an applicator. Those are the kind that my mom uses; you basically jam it there yourself with your fingers. But it's kind of . . . well. Never mind. Do you have any more pads or whatever? I'm guessing you found the stuff at home?"

"Yeah," she said. "No DivaCups, though."

"You are *so* not ready for a DivaCup."

"What was Wade talking about out there?" Daisy asked.

Poppy stopped. Sighed. Snapped the goggles at her hip and wound the straps around her wrist. "Lilah's pregnant."

❖

❖   ❖

Daisy sat at dinner, picking through the boring spinach salad and lentil cakes that Poppy had made. Lilah was humming to herself, pushing around slices of pineapple on her plate, and Poppy kept telling her to stop dicking around with her food and eat it, to which Lilah would say, "I'm not hungry" or "I already ate before"—the kinds of answers a little kid would offer. Daisy could feel Poppy's annoyance from across the table but both Carna and her mother were oblivious. For once, Violet made no effort to include everyone in the conversation. Instead, she and Carna were talking about the estimate for the roof repair in tense, low tones, and as usual, Violet pressed for solutions that annoyed Carna.

"You've got to call him," Violet repeated. "It's not like he's not going to notice."

"I hate to bother him right now, with everything else."

"There's a giant hole where our daughters sleep!" Violet was getting louder.

"Just let me figure it out," Carna said, standing and gathering her utensils to her plate. "I want to at least try to save him some hassle."

"What about our hassle?" Violet pressed, following her into the kitchen. "Lilah was scared shitless!"

"I'm fine, Mother," Lilah huffed, rolling her eyes.

"Glad everyone's so worried about my well-being," Poppy said. "If Daisy hadn't moved my bed to the other wall, I could have been killed."

Carna popped her head out of the kitchen. "For the record, I care about all of us here, equally. And you were passed out on the couch, after waltzing in at three thirty-six a.m., after doing god knows what, but you'll notice I haven't given you any shit about *that*. So spare me, please."

"I was just saying!"

Carna wiped her hands on her jeans. "No, you just want to bitch about how I run things around here, as usual. If you didn't like it, you didn't have to come back for the summer."

Poppy stood up, fists at her sides. Her mouth wobbled like she couldn't decide what to say, and then she went out the front door and slammed it so loud the pictures on the walls swung.

✦

✦

✦

That night Lilah curled into the couch, watching *The Reavers* on Poppy's old laptop, which whirred audibly atop an embroidered pillow. Poppy had tried to get the whole family to watch the show, but only Lilah really liked it. The show was a period piece about a pirate and the woman he loved, a clothing designer in Paris, whom he funded with the booty from his adventures. Daisy had watched the first season but once it was revealed that the pirate and the clothing designer were actually siblings, her interest ended.

Daisy watched her sister watching the show—her knees holding up the pillow and computer, giant pink headphones clamped to her head, face twitching in smiles and frowns and occasional laughter—the screen illuminating her more and more as the light from the windows faded. After washing the dishes, Daisy tried to go upstairs to the ruined attic, but Carna and Violet warned her away.

"It's just not safe," her mother had said, and explained the damage. A gaping hole where the shingles had split, the knee walls buckled. She and Carna had nailed blue tarps over the hole, as the forecast promised more rain. Her mother kissed Lilah on the head and then drifted toward the shower. "All of you just get comfy down here."

"It'll only be a couple of nights," Carna said, as she poured herself a glass of whiskey and took it to the back porch. Daisy slumped down at the table and replied to a text Gretel had sent: a picture of a dog wearing glasses, and then she texted Poppy—*where are u.* She picked at the white threads on her cutoffs until Violet came from the shower smelling like wet flowers. She stopped to smooth Daisy's hair back from her cheek.

"My little Crazy Daisy, would you like some strawberry shortcake?"

"No thanks."

"Okay," her mother said. "I love you. Do you think Lilah wants some?"

"Why don't you ask her?"

"She looks very content just as she is. I know better than to disturb that, by now." Her mother swept into the kitchen, clanking plates and silverware, and then ducked into the back porch with two plates of shortcake. The scent of strawberries was everywhere, and Daisy suddenly felt very afraid. She wanted Poppy to come back. She wanted to pull off Lilah's headphones and ask her, flat out, what had happened. She wanted to go upstairs and inspect the hole, the damage, the tree that had almost killed her sisters. From the outside, the tree was all branches dangling over the eaves like hangnails. She wanted to see where it had pierced the roof and split it open. She listened to her mother and Carna's conversation in the back porch, which sounded careful and measured, aware of being in earshot. They were discussing the things on the other side of the collapsed knee wall—a headboard, a trunk of some sort—and then Violet started in again about how they needed to call Rob Isherwood so he could start an insurance claim. Carna agreed to making the call in the morning, though Violet thought it was irresponsible to wait.

"Jesus, Vi," Carna replied. "They've had a death in the family. The insurance company has to understand. And you think they'll send anyone out right away? With the holiday weekend coming up?"

"Of course they will! That tornado over in Halleck had agents on the scene just hours later. This is a big deal, Carna! It's the literal roof over our heads."

"Spare me the drama."

"No, you want to spare Rob, as usual." Violet's voice got lower. "We offer up all these little inconveniences as a measure of grace, he's a busy man, fine. But this is different. It's stupid and irrational, and you know it."

Daisy's phone beeped with a text. She hoped it was Poppy because the fear growing inside her felt cancerous, malignant. But instead of Poppy responding, it was Hugh:

you should come over

✦ ✦ ✦

Hugh met her by the service road on his four-wheeler by the stand of trees where the NO TRESPASSING sign hung askew from its nail and invited her to get on. She held on to his back as if it were normal to touch him. Gripped him when he sped up. Laughed when he laughed. Prayed no one would see them speeding across the fields. There was no way to tell Hugh to stop or what to do;

for Daisy, there was comfort in knowing that someone else was in charge. There always had been.

But high speeds had never been Daisy's favorite. At this velocity, it was more feeling than seeing: dust everywhere, in her nose, around her ankles and knees, the wind flipping her hair at her temples, Hugh's back sweaty around her fingertips. It wasn't until he turned on the four-wheeler's lights that she realized how long they'd been riding. And that she had no idea what would happen after they quit. They were in the field diagonal from the strawberry patch, and the automatic lights on the outbuildings by Dunedin Towing and Trucking flicked on.

Hugh kept the four-wheeler running but turned off the lights.

"What did you tell your family you were doing?"

"Nothing. Just going for a walk."

"Walking around alone at night's pretty ballsy. You don't even have a dog."

"I like being out at night," she said. Though that wasn't quite true, now it could be. No one had ever called her *ballsy*. She was glad he couldn't see her smiling.

He floored the four-wheeler, bounding across the dirt without lights, going faster than before. Daisy tried not to think about what would happen if they had an accident, about what would happen if Poppy was to find out that she was with Hugh. She hoped she would die, if they crashed.

As they neared the house, Rusty approached, barking and loping beside them, his fur flopping in wiry twists.

He parked behind the garage and helped her off. Rusty snuffled his wet nose against her thigh and she petted him until Hugh whistled at him: "Go on, boy. Get!" Rusty didn't listen but followed them across the yard, away from the Isherwoods' dark house. Halfway to the barn, Hugh spit out his dip and grabbed her hand. His was rough and callused and sweaty. She looked down at her sandals, making sure her footfalls landed somewhere certain in the dark. He paused by a cupboard inside the barn and grabbed some things that clanked and rustled as he tucked them under his free arm. Then he motioned her up the hayloft ladder and she did so, quickly, so he wouldn't see her butt and thighs at that angle for very long.

She stood in the hayloft door again, looking across the dark fields. Green slips of fireflies swirled and tumbled above the corn. She remembered being younger, trying to count them.

"*One . . . twothreefour . . .*"

"*Fivesixseven!*"

"*Eightnine!*"

"*Daisy, you were counting mine!*"

"*How can you tell?*"

Hugh sat with his legs dangling over the edge and she joined him to see what he was opening: a bottle of warm root beer and a package of peanuts from Fleet Farm. She smiled in the dark; her guess would have been that he'd hidden alcohol, that he was keen to drink in the same way he drove the four-wheeler too fast. Guys did that all the time. Got drunk and pissed off—or the reverse—and did terrible things. Started fights. Smashed in windows. Threw rocks at cars until the cops came. Things that were allowed in Hogestyn, but probably not tolerated in a bigger town. The visibility of this anger had always felt staged to Daisy. A kind of unnecessary pose that boys liked, in the same way that Lilah smiled while brushing her teeth or Poppy tilted her head inspecting her makeup in the vanity mirror of the car. All of which were normal, but still poses, Daisy thought. Root beer and peanuts suited Hugh better.

She didn't dangle her legs—not being able to see well made her nervous about heights—but she took a handful of peanuts that she didn't eat. Couldn't eat. She stared down at them and felt panicked. For herself, for Lilah, for Hugh's body half in and half out from this height. For the hole in the roof she was dying to tell him about.

"What's wrong?" he asked, at last.

She shrugged. "Nothing's wrong."

"No," he said. "That's bullshit. Just say it."

She cracked a peanut in half and licked the nut but didn't eat it.

"What if somebody finds us here?"

Hugh's face was hard to read in the dark. But he didn't reply, and for a minute it was just the clicking of peanut shells and the crickets out in the fields.

"She doesn't know anything," he said.

Daisy sighed.

"It's not . . . *Daisy*." He leaned in to stare at her for a moment. "It's not like anything really *happened*."

For a furious, scorching minute, she hated him. So much had *happened* that day. And most of it wasn't anything she could talk about out loud.

She crushed the peanut and the shell and tossed both out the hayloft door. The gesture made her feel babyish, completely and unbearably fifteen years old. Too young to understand what was happening; a runner-up to someone more beautiful, an understudy for a real girl. Hugh was now watching her closely, and she felt certain he would tell her more of how she was wrong.

But as she reached into the plastic sack, Hugh touched her wrist. She let go of the peanuts, and he leaned over and kissed her. Instantly, there was a soaring feeling, the equal, absolute opposite of her fury. Everywhere in her body dilated as she recalled the red-haired woman with no face, the twitch between her legs. Tasting Hugh's mouth, smooth and salty, feeling his whiskery cheeks, hearing the night squeak and chirp far below them was a startling blend of sensations.

They kissed and held hands over the peanut bag and he pushed away from the hayloft door so they could press together better. The leaning toward each other wasn't graceful or comfortable but she didn't care. She would do whatever Hugh wanted, she knew. This was not how she had been raised, this was not how Carna would define a feminist, this was not the kind of ethic Violet would preach. This was an age difference, something bad in Poppy's eyes, an offer only a stupid girl would accept. But it didn't matter. She moved closer and then he was squashing her against him, half into his lap. He pressed her hand on the crotch of his shorts. A minute later, as if she wanted it to be her own idea, her hand began to unbutton and unzip. It dipped under his boxer briefs. He was hard, and she could feel hair; the tip was wet. Her first thought was that being this way must hurt.

She looked up at him, but he was looking down at where her

hand was. She squeezed him and he said, "Oh god," so she squeezed him again. Ran her hand up and down, getting acquainted with the strange way the skin slid over itself. When he moved back to give her more access, she met his eyes for the first time.

"Just like that," he said, then looked down at her hand lost in his boxer-briefs. She kept pulling at him, slowly. He closed his eyes. She didn't look at where her hand bulged underneath his shorts but instead at his face, which was bunched and tense. She hoped he would not open his eyes.

Soon his body jerked and clutched. He said, "Oh," in a long whisper, and then she felt warm streams looping around her fingers.

All the names for this ran through her head. She held on to him for a minute more until he took her hand—her unremarkable hand with its unpainted nails and the healing burr scratch on her index finger—and wiped it on his shorts. She felt very embarrassed for him.

She looked out the hayloft door at the dark fields, toward a stream of headlights far off on an access road near the Dunedins' property. She could hear his zipper go up, and then the rustle of the peanut bag again. She didn't want to meet his eyes.

"You know why your sister dumped me, right?"

She couldn't believe he would ask this, right now. Right after.

"Kind of." She shrugged. She had never seen the dick pic, but she didn't want him to believe for a minute she had, even so.

"It wasn't no goddamn dick pic."

"What was it, then?"

"Pretty basic," he said. "I asked her to marry me."

Chapter Six

The new barn was finished just before midsummer, and that day, we hosted a fine gathering. From all over the county came men and women to celebrate its raising, the sturdy seats of brick, the boards the color of young wine, the white gambrel roof and its matching cupola bright as a baptismal gown. Arthur's pride for this was thick and generous. He tipped his hat toward me as I stood in the yard organizing the ladies and their covered bundles of food. Two hogs from the Haedesch farm were slaughtered for the occasion, and the men waited with jugs of ale while the women set the long tables in the fields, tying the heavy linens around the legs so the tin plates and cups wouldn't fly away in a breeze. Baskets of bread and berries, pitchers of cider, platters of meat and pots of stew. An army of aproned girls set upon the hungry workers as they ate and drank and sweated under the afternoon sun, shouting stories of the proud red triumph rising behind them. It remained empty of animals; Patrick had insisted that they wait to move them until tomorrow. There would be too much fuss for the horses' liking, he said to Arthur Ganey, "Change makes a creature sore and restless," he explained. "And the ladies will not like it if the animals interfere with their feast."

To prepare for this day had meant weeks of work for Maude and me, as well as a fleet of girls loaned to us from neighboring farmsteads. I starched piles of aprons Maude special ordered for each of the ladies so that their good frocks would not be sullied as they served the men. Every morning had brought a host of new tasks—firewood to be gathered, hearths to be swept, flowerpots to be freshened with water, crocks to be wiped and polished. Arthur hired musicians from a county away and they had to be fed and given beds with the other working hands. The fiddler kept loitering around the maids in the kitchen, specifically the Haedesch girl, and Maude was constantly running him off.

By sundown, most of the men were drinking cider in the shade. The women, having tidied the tables, were sewing or stitching on the porch, while maids washed plates and cups behind the main house. The fiddler kept pace with the drunker men who stomped in the dirt behind the new barn, hollering and singing, a prelude to the dancing set to come at twilight. I could see Maude disliked the music; she had wished for the afternoon to be for quilting but none of the women had anything at the ready for such, which she viewed to be a lie told to puncture her pride as hostess. Mistress Hellerstadt attempted to lead the women in song, but many had sleeping babes in arms to tend between tatting and darning socks, the latter of which peeved her. Maude's eyes glided over the homely repair efforts with pouched lips, and I was overcome with weariness. Fury too. The laughter and goodwill fluttering about the farm were a rarity, a delight neither Maude nor Mistress Hellerstadt could generate with their own labor, and I hated that anyone would find a reason to spoil it. I hated that the others followed Maude's lead and called her "Mistress" Hellerstadt, though she was nothing more than the spinster daughter of the rich family who owned the sawmill, who kept rooms above the general store, and who'd once upon a time had a lesson from a traveling contralto who claimed to have studied with Nellie Melba. I knew most would not see me fit for the title, even if I chose to wear it. Not until I brought babies; this I understood and also hated. I set down my stitching and went to the kitchen to wash cups and dry plates so that nobody might sense my thoughts. I preferred courting Maude's irritation at finding me beside the serving girls to sitting in silence while she huffed and groused.

When dusk came, the finer sort of guest had said their farewells. Sleeping children were loaded into carts and wagons amidst empty baskets. The music from behind the barn came louder, for a fire now burned there, banked on the old fence posts yanked and replaced just in time for the gathering. All these details seen to by Arthur and Maude and myself, but now Maude was inside the house, the lamp out, a sign of her displeasure; and Arthur was fully in his cups, drunker than I'd seen him on our wedding night, shirtsleeves rolled to his elbows, face red and laughing in the circle of other drinking men.

I did not mean to join the maids dancing. I feared Maude's upbraiding me at breakfast the next morning. But the Haedesch girl slung an arm around my neck, offering me a cup of cider. It was warm but sweet, bits of clove floating about as acrid as the flames edging up in the fire. I sat on the back steps, hiding from the drunker men, who had blundered into the kitchen only to catch the rough side of Maude's tongue. We giggled, the image of Maude in her night rail, screeching at the bewildered fools. One of the brighter workers came round the house, lighter on his feet than the others, and put out his hand to the Haedesch girl, who rose like a flame toward him and flickered out to the dark beyond the kitchen garden. *Sweethearts*, the others said, heads tilting toward each other like horses. My belly felt seeded with embers, then, and I was aflame with a wanting I couldn't name. Shouted verses floated back to where we hid, and another man whispered, "Come on, ladies, have a turn, none of us bite," and that was all it took. We rushed, a herd of fillies loosening their caps, apron strings flying behind us, toward the music.

I didn't see Patrick at first. I stood aside for many songs, watching the shyer men tap their toes and survey the maids. I watched the girls twirl their skirts and laugh, link arms and spin first with each other, then with some of the bolder men. Cups and bottles of ale passed from hand to hand, ribbons unfurled at the ends of long braids, kerchiefs passed over sweating brows and necks. How lovely to see faces so bright and jolly! No guile, no guilt. Every mouth open in a grin or a laugh. The fiddler's waistcoat swung open as his ringed fingers plucked. All of the jewels paste, surely, but still brilliant in the firelight.

A hand at my waist startled me. "Evening, young missus." Patrick's voice. The heat of his breath curled the hair at my nape.

I did not turn.

"Good evening," I said, my eyes on the dancers.

"It is," he allowed. "A fine day for all to enjoy." His hand slid down, following the curve of my hip. Then, away. He moved closer, his arm brushing my shoulder. He drank from a bottle I'd never seen in the Ganey house. His own supply. Wine, not cider.

"Did you enjoy it?" I said, keeping my eyes on the fiddler's flashing rings.

"Ah, but my work is yet undone," he replied. "Tomorrow shall be long."

I nodded, feeling grim that he could not look ahead with the same pleasure I felt now.

"I should hope you enjoyed what you could, even so," I said.

"Aye," he said. "Though the evening has not yet met its end." He retreated again and I was bereft. Until a moment later, his hand touched my back, then twisted the strings of the apron I had forgotten to take off. All of the maids wore them, still.

"Mr. Casey—" I began, looking down so no one might see my shock.

His hand trailed from the apron's ties up my spine, skipping along my rumpled braid.

"Did you see your husband as he went?"

"Went?"

"Surely you'd have noted him, staggering off like a rutting bull."

"No . . . But where has he gone? Is he ill?"

"He's gone from here, and for us, tonight, that is all the blessing we need know," I heard him take another swallow of the wine.

"Should I worry after him, then? What do you advise, Mr. Casey?"

"You might call me Patrick, young missus," he said. His fingers coasted along the buttons on the back of my dress. "But your husband earns no concern, this night." He pressed the bottle into my palm. "I advise you drink as much as you fancy."

I turned to him but could see nothing of his face in the dark. Just the shape of him, hatless, no coat, his height greater than I recalled the last time we'd spoken alone. The winking brass of his belt, the handle of his knife at his hip.

"And if I don't like the taste of your wine?" I asked, stepping forward until I could see the light in his eyes. I expected to see him grinning, but he was stern as a priest.

"Then you might find courage by some other method," he said. "Pass the bottle to another lucky soul and come find me. If you're so inclined. I believe you know the way."

Chapter Seven

Silent tension reigned for a few days between the Whitsun girls. Then, on the morning of the first of July, as the temperature soared to the mid-nineties, Poppy and Lilah got in a fight that ended with Lilah in tears, holding her stomach and locking herself in the bathroom.

Daisy, returning from her morning trip to the ravine creek, was rummaging for a box of cereal when Poppy came into the kitchen.

"How much money do you have?" Poppy asked.

"About seventy-five bucks."

"Is it in the bank or in cash?"

"Cash. Why?"

Poppy sat down at the table and explained. Poppy was out of the herbs that were the only method of treatment Lilah deemed acceptable to handle "the situation." The herbs made Lilah's stomach ache but they were cheaper than the alternative, which was pills Poppy had already bought, but Lilah wouldn't hear of taking them.

"Is that what you were looking at after the funeral?"

Poppy nodded. "We got them for less than normal, because the organization that sent them classified our family as low-income. They're a good thing to have on hand, though. I mean, you get yourself in this situation, I'm gonna shove them down your throat with a funnel, I swear." She laughed, but Daisy didn't know what to say. She laced up her shoes for the trip into town; Lilah was still crying in the bathroom, a racking, heaving sound. None of them said the word *pregnant*.

"Why doesn't she want to do anything else?" Daisy asked.

"Denial?" Poppy said. "I don't know. Wade told me she tried to get really drunk, the night of the funeral. Like that would do something. And last week, she threw herself down some stairs."

"Where? Here?"

"I don't know," Poppy said. "She told Wade that; he told me. Can you get the cash? Mom and Carna left together but I still need to have Mom's car back soon." Lilah's cries increased in pitch; Poppy groaned and rubbed her forehead. "Jesus Christ."

Lilah had always been a loud sort of crier. Violet had encouraged this, because she saw Lilah's withdrawn silence as a barrier to healing. Lilah would take none of the medications the doctor prescribed, and after several rounds of refusals due to the unnaturalness of pills, Violet relented, trying to support her daughter's choices. But this meant all manner of strange things going on in the last year to pull Lilah out of her gloom: special teas, morning meditations, river stones charged with intentions. Transforming the living room into a dance floor with all the furniture at the walls and Violet entreating them to learn the box step as fiddle music played on an old boom box.

"It'll be wonderful for going to weddings!" Violet had shouted, and Lilah, who at first resisted, stood up and spun around the living room with their mother while Daisy watched from the sofa. Carna shook her head, laughed. On nights when they didn't dance, Violet yanked Lilah from her slumped reading position on the sofa and made her take brisk walks down the snowy road, or she pulled out art supplies and bundles of yarn so they could make lanyards and God's Eyes and draw pictures of their inner selves. She insisted on everyone playing gin every night after dinner, which was the only activity Carna would support, because she could drink while it was happening. It had been all Lilah, Lilah, Lilah this entire year when Poppy had been gone at college. If Lilah started bawling while she was mixing blueberry muffin batter with Violet, that was considered progress. A breakthrough. Feeling the feelings, even if the sound of her sister's crying made Daisy's ribs twitch.

"Come back to me, honey," Violet would soothe as Lilah sobbed, flour all over her apron. "Come back, sweetheart, I am here. It's okay. It's all going to be okay. All will be well."

It had been okay, for a while. Lilah danced and cried and colored pictures and made cinnamon scones and started being social again at school, started smiling at boys in the hallways, giggling and tossing her long white-blond hair around. The hair that made her distinct, that no one else could match for length or color.

But now Daisy could see it was all just a phase. Now Lilah

sounded like she was going to choke, and Poppy's fingers curled around her car keys and she said, "Let's go, Daisy."

Poppy drove through Hogestyn, where fireworks stands were doing brisk business, and the lampposts were swagged with red-white-and-blue banners. Daisy kept quiet. Poppy was angry, plus they were going to Walmart, which she hated, so there were few things Daisy could say that wouldn't result in Poppy shouting. Daisy knew getting shouted at in a Walmart wasn't the worst thing that could happen in that place, but she had learned that sometimes it was better to be quiet and wait. She was curious to see what Poppy would buy. That the things required to unmake a pregnancy would be sold someplace as ordinary as Walmart shocked her.

The moment she put the car in park, Poppy started to speak.

"She doesn't like how her stomach's feeling!" she said, too loud.

"Well, guess what? Imagine how it'll feel full of Tyler Haytch's baby!" she yelled. "Of all people she could have . . . Jesus Christ!"

"Tyler's the father?" Daisy asked.

"Wade hopes not," Poppy said, shutting off the car. "He's not a big fan of his cousin. That whole side of his family, really."

"But Tyler Haytch . . . that's a possibility?"

"He's just one of an illustrious panel of Hogestyn's finest," Poppy said. "She wouldn't say, but Wade said that he heard that after she got out of the hospital, it sort of went around all the guys, how she was up for whatever. I guess she's been pretty busy."

"Busy?"

"That's his word," Poppy said, getting out of the car and

slamming the door. "You know Wade. Treating everyone like ladies or whatever. He can't stand the idea of his Jesus-freak cousin bonging anyone, either. I mean, Wade's far from the brightest bulb in the circuit, but at least he's got that going for him."

In addition to his weird chivalry, Wade wasn't someone who was afraid to act on things. He was protective and loud and didn't care what anyone thought about either of those reactions. Daisy wondered whether Poppy had any idea how much she was like Wade Dunedin. But she saw him as just an embarrassing impediment, a boy like Hugh she'd hoped to shed along with the rest of her small-town skin.

As they walked into Walmart, Poppy ignored the old man offering a cart. She grabbed a basket while Daisy ducked her head down in shame. They had only a little window before Carna needed her car back, and if Violet came home and found Lilah crying in a puddle . . . well. Daisy couldn't decide if it was better to let Carna and Violet know about Lilah's circumstances or just hope Poppy would solve it. Poppy had solved most everything else for them, growing up.

Poppy filled her basket with something odd from every aisle, from pet supplies to the hardware section. Then, cooking utensils and canning jars, a rubber sink stopper and an empty spray bottle. Finally the health and beauty section, where an old lady bent over looking at foot cream and a girl Daisy recognized from school, but whose name she didn't know, rummaged through perfume testers. A little kid sitting in a shopping cart sucked her thumb, no parents in sight. Poppy stopped in the family planning section, which was in direct view of the pharmacy, and grabbed a pregnancy test in a set of two.

"Why two?"

"It never hurts to have one around."

"Doesn't your mom have any in the house?"

"Her clients generally know they're knocked up by the time they call her." She continued past the condoms and lubricants toward the tampons, grabbing a sack of overnight maxi pads. Daisy felt a small bite of shame. A few nights before, she'd bled out all over her pajamas; she hadn't known there was such a product—a revelation that had made Poppy only more exasperated.

She followed Poppy into the next aisle of giant tubs of protein powder and fitness bars and they squatted down to survey the labels and prices of various strange vitamins. Daisy finally asked what had been on her mind, the thing she had feared to bring up.

"Why can't we just tell them?"

"Because Lilah won't do what they ask, anyway," Poppy said, glancing around. "You know how she is about pills. All her stupid bullshit about fucking modern medicine! And neither of our moms has a pot to piss in, if you haven't noticed. I could barely afford them, myself. Which is why I got you involved, really. Money. Because this shit is not anything you should be dealing with, Daisy."

"They could figure it out," Daisy said, a bit annoyed that her sister thought her so inept. "Carna got all our vaccines once, from that one doctor, remember?" Daisy recalled them all standing in a line in the kitchen, eyes squinched in fear as Carna jabbed each of them in the arm with the HPV vaccine; the insurance Violet had through her seminary didn't cover that. "I'm sure Carna knows someone who—"

"Not around here," Poppy said. "We'd have to drive at least four hours. You got gas money for that?"

Daisy didn't reply. All the money she had in the world was in the pocket of her shorts right now.

"And I just . . ." Poppy paused. "I just can't hear my mom's bullshit 'I told you so' right now. Or Violet's breathing over everything, making us create a circle of trust or whatever. Neither of them has the thing that matters, which is cash," she said, tumbling another bottle into the basket. "Though the fucker who knocked her up is the one who should be paying for this."

Daisy tried to think of the guys Lilah talked to at school this spring, when she was finally coming out of her daze. They were older and younger, tall and short, cute and ugly and zitty and nerdy and bulky. They all blended into a blur. The only one she could picture was Tyler Haytch. He lived not too far from Old Blackmun Road, but it might have been in another country, still. He was in Lilah's grade, but he was one of those kids who had a pile of siblings that all looked like him, an army of bland boys with buzzed haircuts and camo shorts and tidy polo shirts. Wade's mother was a Haytch, and when she married into the lapsed-Catholic Dunedin family, her family hadn't approved. Neither family was big on the other, and after Wade's parents divorced and Mrs. Dunedin remarried, there was no reason for keeping up appearances. The Haytch family wasn't as rich as the Isherwoods, but they did well enough at hog farming that Mr. Haytch donated a pile of money to build his brother a big church in an industrial chicken barn out on the highway. Though the Haytch kids didn't go around praying in the cafeteria, the family was pretty religious—Mrs. Haytch put up a large sign with a cross that said ABORTION KILLS BABIES by their mailbox, which was often the subject of graffiti: over the years the sign had also proclaimed that GODZILLA KILLS BABIES or DRAGONS KILLS BABIES. Mrs. Haytch wrote letters to the Hogestyn newspaper complaining about it but never stopped repainting the sign and posting it back up.

"But if it's too late, then what are we going to do?"

Poppy looked through her basket full of bottles and pads and some kind of liquid with a label Daisy couldn't see. "We're going to see if any of this works," she said. "A girl I know on my floor did it, and she was okay. It's a lot less than what we'll be in for at a clinic."

"But if this—" Daisy nudged the basket between them. "What if this doesn't do it?"

"Then we're going to be aunties to some dumb-ass dickheads' baby," Poppy said. "Get it now?"

✦ ✦ ✦

A couple nights later, after Daisy got out of the shower and was in fresh pajamas, when she went to the back porch to sleep, Carna and Rob Isherwood were sitting there, two juice glasses of whiskey between them and pile of paperwork beside Carna's ashtray.

"Oh, sorry," Daisy said, stepping back, not wanting to be near Hugh's dad in her sleep shorts that were too small to be seen anywhere in public and which had little jack-o'-lanterns on them.

Carna glanced up, but didn't yield the space, though Mr. Isherwood said hello. Carna ignored Daisy and resumed talking about the tree service. Daisy fled to her mother's room, where Violet was sorting through her closet, her mouth in a frown.

"I have no patriotic clothing, Daisy," she said, as if this were a shocking announcement.

"What?"

"I own white clothes and blue clothes, but nothing red," she said. "I'm going to look a little dismal for the fireworks tomorrow."

"You're going to the fireworks?"

Violet examined a light pink shirt as if it would possibly pass for red. "I have to present an award to the Coughlins for their blood drive. If you want to come with, the church is bringing a group in one of the vans . . ."

"Maybe," Daisy said, knowing immediately she would never go to any event that involved her mother's church van. Such outings usually required unloading and loading, of either people or heavy equipment, and there were always a bunch of stops—little kids being dropped off, old people being walked to their doors. Once a child had an allergic reaction at a picnic and the van had been diverted to urgent care. "Fireworks aren't my favorite."

"They never have been, have they?" her mother said, touching Daisy's cheek. Violet's hair needed a trim and her eyes creased as she smiled. "Lilah likes them, though."

"Yeah, for some reason, she does," Daisy replied. "She probably has something red to wear." Lilah wasn't a fan of church van trips, either, but she loved the summer rummage sales Violet's congregation organized each spring. She and Poppy always pillaged through what didn't sell and remade things to fit their needs, Poppy because she wanted to be stylish beyond the confines of what Hogestyn's meager retail scene could offer, and Lilah because she had always been a fan of dress-up. She had two dressers full of clothing—one that contained what she actually wore and another to store scraps and bits for costumes and other inventions. This was the one interest where Lilah and Poppy collided. Both of them had learned to sew from their mothers, using the vintage turquoise Singer machine from Grandma Whitsun.

Her mother hugged her. Daisy was consumed with her scent. Basil from the garden and tonight's marinara sauce, the vague florals of her shampoo, which was a golden bottle specifically formulated for blond hair that she and Carna both liked, and a faint bleach from her white shirt. "I think Lilah is doing so much better, don't you," her mother whispered.

"Yes."

"The funeral made me nervous," she said. "I thought it might be too much for her."

"I think she handled it all right."

"Me too." Her mother kissed her head and then her cheek. "We need more time together. Let's make a date, you and I, all right?"

Daisy nodded. Dates with her mother were just little outings to the coffee shop or the grocery. The two of them buying ice cream or lattes and then noodling around for a little while. Daisy liked this; historically, it had made her feel special and specific, someone distinct from her older sisters and the larger concerns of Violet's church members. But the idea of being alone with her mother with the freight of all these new secrets now frightened her. Telling the truth about Lilah would mean shattering the contentment Violet had just quietly pronounced. It would mean another crisis, another series of lessons for future sermons. It would mean Violet would someday narrate how the day before America's holiday, she had held her youngest and spoken aloud words that would later prove to be gravely wrong. And Daisy would sit in the pew and relive this moment of basil and bleach and flowers and whispers.

She had relived lots of things this way: the death of Grandma Whitsun, from a liver damaged by alcoholism (that meditation was about redemption and hope); the ripple effect of loss (about her own father, whom she'd never met); about the simple joys of everyday life (all three of them as little girls, running around naked in the yard, screaming through the sprinkler just as the mail carrier arrived). The essentials of Daisy's life reduced to plots and props and settings, each with an easy moral to take away. People loved the Reverend Whitsun's sermons; they loved her kindness and openness. There was no way to rebel against this. Even Violet's letting her daughters decide when and where to attend services, what to believe in and investigate, was a type of gentleness. Even when she tried to escape notice, rush through the brush down to the coolness of the ravine and its shallow icy creek, Daisy was just another story to her mother. A lesson in nature soothing our wild hearts, a testament to silence and wonder, a way to bear witness to the mysteries inside us.

Later, after Carna had swept the whiskey glasses and ashtray from the porch table, and Daisy had clipped a reading lamp to the back of the chaise lounge, she lay under the quilt, listening to the sounds of her family. Carna was brewing coffee—a client had just started laboring, but it was her fourth child and didn't need attention yet—and making sandwiches for what lay ahead. Violet was doing a puzzle at the table with Lilah while listening to old country-music records. Both Lilah and Daisy loved these records, but Poppy hated them, pointedly wearing headphones while she ironed out the old sheets they'd found in the trunk behind the destroyed knee wall. Carna had told her to hand-wash them, then line-dry them. The trunk was lined in cedar so everything inside was still intact, nearly fresh, considering its age. The whole house now smelled of cedar and old starch. In between songs on the record, Daisy could hear the iron's steaming hiss.

She shivered beneath the quilt; a new wave of storms rumbled above in the dark. She shut off the reading lamp, let her book thud to the floor. Closed her eyes and remembered eating peanuts with Hugh in the hayloft. The root beer, the firefly light, the way his face looked as she clutched at him beneath the easy give of his underwear. She couldn't believe he'd asked Poppy to marry him. Nobody did that anymore: married right out of high school, if they weren't pregnant. Even if they were. Not even the Haytch brothers did that, though Daisy recalled that one of them, the eldest, was now engaged. There was a picture in the newspaper of him and his fiancée looking at each other with her ring showing, standing beneath a lattice arbor in the park across from the library. But they were older, twenty-six or twenty-seven. The girl worked as a receptionist for a printing company and the Haytch kid was a manager at Tires Plus. They were going to get married in the chicken-barn church the uncle ran and though they seemed as religious as the rest of the family, they'd waited a decent interval after high school. What was Hugh's deal? That Poppy had lied about this in the first place made no sense, either. A dick pic, a ridiculous marriage proposal—either would have taken nothing more for Poppy to mock it.

Beyond the porch, owls called to each other. The squeak of the ironing board folding, the splatter of puzzle pieces spilling back into the cardboard box, the backward scrape of the record player needle being guided to its rest. Yawns, soft words, the sounds of pillows being punched and blankets spread over the sofa. Her mother in the bathroom, splashing water on her face and then the scent of her coconut face cream. The Whitsuns had never been a family heavy with marriages and weddings, with men. Her grandma Whitsun had never married the man who was Carna and Violet's father; they lived together without contract until he joined the army and came back married to a woman from somewhere else. Violet had married Daisy's father, but that had been in front of a judge, and even so, it proved to be doomed. Her dead father's own father was a phantom, too; he'd died of a stroke when her father was about her age. And of course, Carna had never been forthcoming about who had fathered Poppy. Any mention of it brought nothing factual. A reference to parthenogenesis, of Athena springing from Zeus's brain, and an explanation of how that myth was masculinized, distorted, all of which was meant to dazzle the questioner with facts they hadn't asked for. This was probably why people talked about her family like they were a band of hippie witches. Why people like Tyler Haytch called them slutty trash. Those were the words Wade meant when he called Lilah *busy*.

The kitchen light snapped off, and Daisy was in total darkness. Carna came out to the porch, pulling her wheeled suitcase where she kept all her birth supplies, a tiny cooler of food under her arm, and a thermos of coffee in her other hand. A pack of cigarettes was stuffed in her front shirt pocket.

"You awake still?" Carna said, her voice at a low tone that told Daisy that the others were asleep.

"Yeah."

"Put the latch on the back door after I leave," she said.

"Okay."

"Sleep well."

"You too," Daisy said.

"Ha," Carna said. "Not likely. See you tomorrow, kid."

Chapter Eight

The house they made of Patrick's stable is bigger than his modest hut he loved so well, but it pressed upon the youngest girl. She bursts out the doors like someone underwater gasping up to the surface. She climbs over trees that once stood when I was able to climb. She rushes past brambles and spikes of thistle, stomping over the secret spots where Patrick laid snares. She follows the same path each day in summer, down to the ravine where I had thought the river woman lived. There, a creek pulses with the coldest, sweetest water; that she puts her feet in such water would be a blasphemy but for the futile labor of dragging a full bucket up the incline. Patrick washed his body here, but I never did. Despite visiting all the places he knew, I have no reach of him. His end is lost to me. Perhaps he died in some other place I cannot visit. Perhaps the devil took all of him, man and memory. Perhaps that is another punishment I earned: the full bounty of Maudé's and Arthur Ganey's memories. Cruel that I am only allowed to see them fully now, when they are gone.

What I knew of Patrick Casey was only what I acquired as a living girl. The first fact of him: He had been just as lonely as I was. That first night I came upon him, I could see how his body yearned and bent for company. He was too proud a man to say so. And, for all his posing, he was not much more of a man than I was a woman. He was nineteen years when he pulled me from the water, though his nineteen years had been filled with more than eerie village stories and pretty sewing.

From Patrick, I learned not only how much I had lost but how little I had acquired of this world. I learned that it hadn't been just death or peril at sea or leaving home that gutted me, that sent me toward the edges of the Ganey farm seeking more than blooms and berries. It was learning that what I conceived of as the whole world was merely a marble, compared to the knowledge of this boy, who lived in a hut on a rich man's land, beside a rich man's horses, who said he had crawled his way up the Mississippi on rafts and riverboats, collecting languages to mix with his curses and brogue. He told his origins differently each time. He was the son of a priest, he said, grinning at the scandal. Daring me to call out the lies, which I never did; they were his sport. Born of a healing woman amongst wagons on Little Christmas, born in the stables behind a brothel, born shipwrecked, at low tide. The many makes of Patrick Casey. A christened Catholic, a pagan baby, a card player tossing skirts and dice. All tales I accepted but none of which I needed to believe.

What I could believe of him was only what he did with his hands. Fashioned bricks from mud and buttons from wood, twisted whips from leather scraps, brushed horses, shoveled fresh hay, hauled water from the creek in the valley, the same place he washed each morning with soap of lard and lemon balm. He'd never had a home before he built the one he now lived in, all for himself. A low man, the people of my village might have said. A wily chancer. Not a lad for my father's girls, come to court with flowers after mass, hat in hand. My mother's people would not have greeted his lot in the lane, despite the madness that twined through their line like serpents.

But Patrick did not know what I had been. He knew my grief from the sad report I offered in the Finn's boat—"I am Jane. I am the only one." Apart from these facts, naught mattered. He did not care that my talents were few beyond fine stitches, creasing shirts, or setting a table. He did not care that I was another man's. Like all young men, he did not preoccupy himself with consequence. The only legacy he minded was his own.

This place wasn't like the village back at home, he said. This place is one where a man may come and go. "Once you have what you need, you don't ask, you don't tell the priest, you stand up and leave. In America, a man can be done with forgiveness."

◆

◆

◆

"Take your hair down, lass."

"Stop calling me 'lass'—you sound like that fiddling fool."

"Please."

"I will not. It will get bits of straw in it and the Haedesch girl will find them when she shakes out my bedding."

"Then I will search each and every hair on your head before you take your leave of me."

"We haven't time for such, and you know it."

"We haven't time, and that is why I ask it. You have not visited for days."

"Maude's parlor has been well appointed of late. Mistress Hellerstadt is giving singing lessons."

"That woman's voice could choke a rat."

"It is good that you are not invited to listen."

"That I would know each hair on your pretty head, Jane Murphy. I would be the God of your entire body."

"You are forthright and possessive of that which you cannot have."

"But don't I? I recall having it many times now."

"Devil."

"Live in my heart and pay no rent."

"Stop."

"Never. I will never."

✦

✦

✦

The second fact: Patrick had killed a man. He spoke this quietly, no boasts or jests. No one would mourn the dead man; he had no regret. Unlike the stories of the river and his humble birth, he did not say this to spin a tale. He laid it out beside his other skills; it had been a simple act, a verdict he arrived at quickly.

When I asked if this was why he came to live in the woods of the Ganey farm, he said the law did not seek him. The river covers

many crimes, he explained. For that he was thankful.

"You do not fear God's judgment?" I asked.

"He has not worried himself over me and mine," he said. "We are at an understanding,"

"Ah. You have made an agreement at a crossroads?"

"The devil draws up contracts there, not our Lord, young missus," he said. He laughed. "But fear not. I make arrangements for my own soul. Yours, too."

"Have you? Does a woman need not be present at such an assembly?"

"You are mistress of a large estate," he said. "'Tis not easy to secure moments of your time."

"You jest. Maude Ganey shall always be mistress here."

"Always' is an oath that tempts deviltry," he said. "Better that a mortal not use it often."

I kissed him then and teased the end of his beard with my fingertips. "You tell me you have taken another's life, and then warn of deviltry? And men say women speak nonsense."

"I cannot speak for all men, but I will speak nonsense as far it keeps you beneath me."

"Ah, but it is you that is beneath me at present."

"The luck is all mine." His hands soothed my back where it ached from the day's washing, and he resumed his serious tone. "You jest. But bedding another man's wife is a grave matter," he continued. "Far more likely to be discovered than the corpse of the bastard who crossed me as a stripling. Would not do to leave its details untended. The hereafter is said to be a long rest. I intend it to be as splendid as I've earned."

◆ ◆ ◆

That was a space of summer, a time now that trips over the three moons like clumsy feet. A time of two marriages. One within the pages of the Ganey Bible, neat as clean pins in a sewing basket, and the other without, open to the night on straw-covered horse blankets, secret oaths lit by no lamps but the banked fire and the stars of God's heaven.

Mornings thereafter, I would rise in my empty bed and feel alive, despite my broken sleep. I would wash and dress and take my breakfast with Maude, who ruled the kitchen, her one grim pleasure. On fair days, I would boil water for laundry and dunk every sullied scrap in the house, beating out the stains, rinsing the cloth with water so cold it made me gasp, then pinning it all up to bake fresh in the sun.

Maude had five lines tacked between the summer kitchen and the house. Though the Haedesch girl had always done the washing, I insisted this be my task and sent the girl to mind the chickens instead. Maude said this was not work for women such as us, though she deigned to know exactly how each chore must be accomplished, harassing the Haedesch girl to tears some days over folded napkins and tarnished silver. As far as I saw it, Maude had never been a girl tossed into stormy waters; she struck me as the sort who had been given most things. She only wanted me for the one task she herself could not accomplish. She saw I could not turn her brother's head, and so, I might well ruin my hands in cloudy suds and chap my fair face in the sun as I scrubbed the dirt from her stockings.

But Maude was clever to skirt the washing as she did. Laundry is hard work. A shirt, as light as a feather once kissed by strong winds, feels as thick as an anchor when drenched in a bucket. Still, I missed having the water as a neighbor. I longed for the smell of salt air and the sound of waves, constant as my own heart's beating. Enclosed by bedsheets, I could not see the fields that expanded black and green in all directions. Gone were the barns and trees and mules dragging stumps out of the soil so that axes could chop them to kindling for our winter stoves. Gone were the whispering grasses and trees, the buzzy call of bees milling about the flowers Maude tended on the porch and the window boxes. I was a hidden girl in a world of my making, skirts and chemises and night rails, flimsy drawers to which I had added lace and colored flowers before Maude told me to stop.

"Jane, must I say it again? We are not that *sort*," Maude sniffed, standing above me as I sewed in the last bits of lamplight one evening. I did not touch her clothes with my needle afterwards. But inside my linen keep, I was able to look at what I liked, dream what I pleased, recall the night in Patrick's hut long after the fire died and the music stopped. The sounds of hands on skin. The touch of a tongue to my knee, to my thigh, to the tender place along my ribs.

"Lord, but the look of you," he had said, his body rising above mine, his chest smooth and bare in the lantern light. The trail of stitches knotting along damp linen, reveries in yellow, blue, green, pale rose. His mouth divine on mine. His hands clutching my hip, trembling. Wine and cider and the ghost of music playing in my head as he gasped and spent on my thigh. My hair falling around us. The cold water dripping from my fingers as I squeezed and shook out skirts and napkins.

"Nothing is finer than this," he said, his fingertips skating across my breast, up my neck, pausing at my cheek. "The devil's magic is God's best work." I had no words; my breath was rough. There was nothing but his face, his hands, the scent of straw and animals. The fire crackling in the grate.

I snapped out each bit of cloth unto which I'd pricked out the messages of my dreams in the dying light of each day until they reeled out toward the sky, then pinned all these glories that touched the parts of me only Patrick knew onto the steady ropes that bound this world, pretty flowers and shooting stars, little rows of ducklings and birds in trees, colors nobody could see in the dark.

Chapter Nine

Wade picked them up as soon as Violet left for church. Daisy had wanted to walk, but Lilah was feeling sick to her stomach and Poppy just wanted to get on with things.

"Get your fill of nature some other time," she snapped. "Walk out the door and breathe in all that manure if you want. You don't have to help with this, you know."

Daisy knew. She had gone over it with Poppy, but still couldn't find a way to be comfortable about being excluded from what was going to happen. How Poppy framed it, the whole thing was the consequence of not having anyone with sense in charge. Had Poppy been around, there would have been no dancing, no meditation, no refusing pills like a toddler clamping up over a spoonful of mushed peas. Had Poppy been around, she would have seen Lilah swanning about in the hallways, in tears one moment and rabidly flirting the next, and she would have known. She wouldn't be stuck trying to induce a miscarriage at Wade Dunedin's house on the one night neither Violet nor Carna was around. In Daisy's head, another word flapped just out of view; she refused to say it.

It was Carna who was messing up the plans for Lilah, anyway. Her client wasn't supposed to deliver this early; Poppy had banked on the woman lingering longer in labor. After much texting, Carna explained she was going to stay on in a postpartum doula role, as there was no family around on the holiday weekend to pitch in. That her mother didn't know when she'd be home had Poppy in a frenzy, finally calling Wade to ask if they could do everything at his house. Mr. Dunedin had filled in on a haul to Texas the day before so there was nobody around.

Nobody, except for two guys in the backyard by an old camper, grilling a beer-can chicken over a tiny Weber grill and drinking Hamm's from a Styrofoam cooler.

"Who the hell is that?" Poppy snapped, as Wade guided the truck toward his house.

"Ah, just my uncle Jay and one of his buddies," Wade said.

"I thought you said no one was going to be home."

"I did. And they're not. He lives in his camper, not in the house, Jesus, could you stop acting like the world's ending?"

"I don't want anyone finding out about this," Poppy said. "It's nobody's business."

"He's my drunk uncle Jay; who's he gonna tell?" Wade asked, shoving out of the truck and extending a hand toward Lilah. "He only comes in the house to shower, and that's not even every week."

"Gross," Poppy said, grabbing her big bag of supplies.

The Dunedin house was a big, sprawling rambler and looked

mostly the same as it had when Wade's mother was married to his dad. Mrs. Dunedin had moved to Georgia last year when Wade graduated, to be nearer her new husband's ailing mother. Since the divorce, the house had lost its gingham café curtains and giant jars of candy-apple-scented candles, but had acquired a giant television and a new sectional sofa. Most of the clutter remained the same. Beer bottles stood on the counter beside the sink, a laundry basket full of socks and T-shirts blocked the hallway. The walls were empty and newly painted, bare of the lineup of family photos and wreaths of dried flowers. Wade led Lilah to the kitchen table, asked if she'd like something to drink.

"Wait," Poppy said. "Let's do this first, and then she can have a drink."

Wade opened the giant stainless-steel refrigerator. An entire shelf was cans of Coke and Budweiser. "We got pop, if you want," he said. "And some juice I think. Fruit punch." Poppy asked him for a spoon and to boil up some water for tea.

Daisy sat on the edge of the sectional sofa.

"Like, in the microwave?"

"You don't have a teakettle?"

Wade sighed.

"Just boil some water in a pan on the stove, then," Poppy said. "It's the same."

"Just plain old shitty water?" Wade said. "Or should I run it through a coffee filter first?"

Lilah turned away to smirk toward Daisy as Poppy huffed around and heated the water herself. Wade joined Daisy on the sofa, clicking on the television through a series of impossibly long remote controls. A giant picture of race cars speeding around a track exploded loudly into the room, but Wade didn't even blink. He handed the remote to Daisy and showed her the button to change the channel, and then went back to the kitchen.

"Should I order some pizza or something?" he asked.

"What for?" Poppy asked, unfolding a square of paper instructions and smoothing it on the table.

"Because it's food?" he said. "And maybe you guys are hungry?"

"Pizza sounds good," Lilah said. She was meeker than usual, tiny at the giant table covered in mail and car magazines.

"I don't want you to eat anything until we get all this inside you," Poppy said.

"Why not?" Wade asked.

"I don't want her to throw it up," Poppy said. "I want to make sure it all stays down."

"Okay," Wade said. "But if I order something now, it'll be a while before it's here."

"True," Poppy said, pulling out two coffee mugs. One said I'M THE BOSS, HOSS and the other was a DUNEDIN TRUCK & TOW mug with the lightning logo that was on all of their trucks and Wade's jacket. "Get something without meat."

"Lilah, you don't eat meat?"

"I do, but lately it sounds awful," Lilah said.

Wade nodded and then pulled his phone out of the pocket of his shorts. "I'll order a double cheese. What else do you like?"

He and Lilah went back and forth over the pizza toppings.

Then, looking up from her instruction sheet and putting her bag of supplies around one wrist, Poppy poured a glass of water and asked where the bathroom was. Wade pointed, and with that, Poppy ushered Lilah down a hall. When she heard a door softly close, Daisy pressed the channel button. A boxing match, a woman cooking mushrooms, a lion jumping toward a herd of wildebeests, a news bit about the opioid crisis. The Whitsuns never had cable, and once the television they had broke, they hadn't replaced it. Rob Isherwood installed internet for them, and Poppy's laptop provided all the shows they needed. But Daisy was hypnotized by the size of the Dunedins' screen. The colors were so rich they almost looked three-dimensional, and the sound came from every part of the room. She fell into show after show, a minute at a time. When she was bored or a commercial came on—or ended, and the show returned—she would push the button and move on to the next surprising thing. Toothpaste, medical lawsuits, dog food, mascara, drag queens posing on runways, food competitions, home remodeling, cartoons.

When she next turned back to her sisters in the kitchen, Poppy was opening pizza boxes. Wade stood beside Lilah, his hair wet from the shower, a towel around his neck, his giant chest bare. Lilah was drinking something from a mug, her mouth alternately a smile and a grimace.

"What are we doing now?" Daisy asked, edging toward the pizza. They almost never ordered pizza. Daisy hadn't even heard the delivery person ring the bell, or noticed who paid.

"Just waiting," Poppy said. "It's all done."

"What?"

Lilah set down her mug. "Well, I have to keep drinking this nasty tea, according to Poppy. Or else it's time for the tubing and the speculum. Also, I might just shit my pants, too. So buckle up. I'm gonna be a Shitsy Kitty."

Wade laughed around a large bite of pizza.

"That might happen," Poppy said. "It might not, though."

"Well, good thing I'm here and not at my own house?" Lilah said, her face pink and angry.

"The bathroom is right by our moms' rooms," Poppy said. "You want them asking what's wrong if you're constantly in there, flushing the toilet for hours?"

"We got two bathrooms," Wade said, grabbing another slice of pizza. "One on both floors."

"See?" Poppy said. "Nobody to bother you. Full luxury here at the Dunedins."

"I don't know about that," Wade laughed. "The basement shitter is awful. Doesn't even have a door."

"Why would anyone use a bathroom with no door?" Daisy asked.

"Ask my drunk uncle," Wade said. He moved away from the counter and dug a shirt out of the laundry basket. "He's pretty much the only one that desperate."

"Gross," Poppy said. She slid a piece of pizza onto a plate and asked Wade where the forks were. "Why can't he get his own place?"

"He used to have one," Wade said. "But then he bought out my grandpa's Christmas tree farm in Halleck, and the whole thing went tits-up in two seasons. So my grandma didn't leave him shit when she died. My dad knows he's a total drunk and probably worse, but he feels sorry for him, so just lets him live on the property. He doesn't really have anywhere else to go."

"I feel like I might barf," Lilah said.

"Do it in the sink," Poppy said, while Wade said, "I'll get you a bowl."

They all stood frozen and ready while Lilah closed her eyes, gripped the counter on either side of the sink. "Okay," she said after a minute. "I'm okay. But . . . I want to sit down."

"Of course," Wade said, leading her to the sofa. Poppy got a bowl from the cupboard. "Do you need a blanket? Are you too cold?" Wade asked.

"I'm a little sweaty,"

"I'll turn up the AC."

"Do you want to watch a movie or something?" Poppy asked. She put down the red plastic bowl on the floor, grabbed the remote, and stared at all the colored buttons in confusion. "I mean, maybe Wade can find something to take your mind off everything."

"Sure," Wade said, moving faster than Daisy had ever seen him. "We've got basically everything. Plus pay-per-view."

After a minute, Wade had found an episode of *The Reavers*, and Lilah sat between him and Poppy like a sick child. Wade slid his arm over the top of the sofa and Poppy brushed back Lilah's hair. The air-conditioning made Daisy's arm hair stand up; it was almost obscenely cold. She imagined Wade and his dad after a long, hot day of driving trucks and towing stranded people, coming back to this giant bosom of a sofa and this precise, perfect chill. In this kind of comfort, even Poppy appeared to have softened.

The episode Wade had picked was the one where the pirate and the fashion designer finally kiss, only to discover a few scenes later that they are brother and sister, which was Daisy's least favorite part of the series. Of course, another two seasons would pass before their true parentage would be revealed but all of it made Daisy fidget. What she had thought this night would be was nothing she had imagined. If she had asked Poppy for specifics, she might have understood and maybe not even come along. But she had been afraid to know exactly what would happen.

She ate some more pizza, then tidied up the kitchen, even though most of the mess had preceded them and she wasn't sure where everything should go. Lilah got up once to use the bathroom and Poppy went with her, Wade waiting on the sofa with the TV on pause.

"Kinda weird, huh?" he said to Daisy.

"Yeah," she said. "Boring, too."

"I hope it stays that way," he said, glancing to the door. "But don't worry. If things go wrong, I don't care what Poppy says, I'm calling an ambulance. Taking her to the ER. Not gonna act like it's no big deal. Okay?"

"Okay," Daisy said. "Thank you. And thank you for the pizza. And that show. It's Lilah's favorite."

"She did a whole report on it in Oral Communications," Wade said. "She was pretty into it."

"I can't stand it," Daisy said.

"Well, yeah," Wade said. "Not really my thing. But it's probably better I sit here and help out instead of stomping a mudhole in my cousin's dumb ass."

"Don't tell Poppy you want to do that."

"Too late," he said. "And I know, Lilah told me she wasn't sure it was him. She was so drunk when she told me! God! She made me promise not freak out, like ten times. I didn't freak out, but I didn't keep the secret. So, I guess I gotta respect her wishes. Though, I'd want to know, if it was me. I'd want to be there, you know. Do something. Be around. I dunno."

"Be a dad?"

"God," Wade said, his face going sour. "I hope not. But you can't just, like, leave a girl on her own. It's not just her problem, right? I mean, it *is*, yeah. But you can't just sit there and expect her to clean it all up by herself. There's other things a guy could do, you know?"

Daisy had no idea what he meant. It wasn't likely that Tyler Haytch or any of the other faceless boys would give Lilah money for an abortion, even if they'd known. That Tyler had even touched Lilah to start with, risking his soul and reputation, was hard to accept. She couldn't imagine him having any kind of concern for any girl in Lilah's position.

"You didn't have to clean up our house, Daisy," he said. "I mean, there's a TV in my dad's room, if you'd rather watch something else. You're welcome to it."

Watching TV where Mr. Dunedin slept: another thing she couldn't imagine. Just then Lilah and Poppy returned.

"Barf?"

"No," Poppy said. "But it's starting," Lilah's face looked rubbed raw, like she'd been crying.

"What do we do?" Wade asked, moving over so Lilah could fit back into the nook between him and Poppy.

"Nothing," Poppy said. "But Daisy needs to call Violet," she added. "She just tried both of us. Where's your phone?"

"I left it at home."

"Jesus! What the hell!"

"Easy, already," Wade said. Lilah looked diminished next to him on the sofa, her features sweaty and green.

"Go home, get your phone, call her," Poppy said. "She's wondering about Carna, can't get ahold of her. Tell her we're hanging out at Wade's for the night."

"For the night? What . . ."

"Tell her it's a campout, and lots of Lilah's friends are coming," she said. "Fireworks. Make it sound fun. Grab the sleeping bags; they're in the closet by the washing machine. Say Wade has an extra tent."

"I do, actually," Wade said, sounding pleased at how nicely Poppy's lie fit.

"What if she comes over here?"

"Why would she?" Poppy asked. "It's not like it's that weird of a situation."

"It's a little weird," Wade allowed. "You never hung out with us after Hugh—"

Poppy cut him off. "Just go and do this, please, Daisy? If it all goes sideways, fine. But right now, things are happening and I can't deal with it. Not for a while. We need the time, all right?"

"Fine," Daisy said.

"Call if anything changes," Poppy hollered. Daisy nodded, then made her steps toward the door just partially reluctant and slow. She didn't want her sisters to know how easy it was for her to leave them behind. How it was not a hardship or a chore. Not even the littlest bit. She ran all the way down the road, her body rejoicing in sweat when she saw that Carna was not yet home. She sprinted inside, grabbed her phone from where it had been charging in the kitchen, and dialed her mother, who picked up in such a breathless, distracted manner that Daisy knew the lie would be easy. She explained the situation, listening to what sounded like a parade in the background. Her mother said she might be late, and Carna was likely to spend another night in Halleck, so what a good thing it was, to have a campout. "How fun!" she said. "Lilah's getting into camping," she murmured to herself. "She's got more of her father than I thought. Kind of amazing, isn't it, Daisy?"

The house was sullenly hot, compared with the Dunedins', and Daisy wished she could hang up, but she let her mother continue to marvel as whatever Fourth of July chaos raged around her, and said they'd be home in the morning. Once she ended the call, she stopped and poured a tall glass of water and drank it entirely. Wiping her brow with a dish towel Carna had embroidered with chickens and a rooster, she sent several texts to Poppy, relaying the basic details, Carna in Halleck, Violet delighted, everything okay.

THANK GOD, Poppy texted back.

No, thank me, Daisy thought. She refilled the glass of water and, halfway through gulping it down, knew exactly what to do next.

Chapter Ten

I do not miss the heat. I do not miss perspiration staining my neckline, undoing my hair from its cap, my thighs chafing from the stockings I hated to wear. Maude insisted that we keep what she called "our civilizing influence" as ladies. We were not to be overrun by male shoddiness as had happened on the Haedesch farmstead, which she considered a boar's nest since Mrs. Haedesch died the winter before I arrived.

"Men need our steady hands," she said. "Just as we need their strong backs. Our comportment must provide a better example."

Maude's better example rubbed and vexed so that my knees and thighs were red and tender. The sweat fouling my clothing undercut Maude's vision of me as the mistress of the Ganey farm nearly as much as her high-handedness about teatime and polished cutlery. I would not ask for new garments nor the cloth to create them. I had no talent in dressmaking; I knit stockings and shawls, I decorated caps with lace and hems with flounces. It had been Bess who had excelled in dressmaking; she had been the one who made our clothes. Once the dresses I had frayed, there would be no more. Each hot day, I became more and more spiteful. That spite still lingers.

But I miss the cold. I long for the bundling of quilts and bodies, the safety of sealed doors and windows, the heat of a fire flushing through a room. When the summer began to fade, my reasons for being out of doors were fewer, and the more I was forced to rub along with Maude and Arthur—pushing around the table, colliding in doorways—the sweeter the moments I found with Patrick. His chimney was new and the bricks fine and strong; our bodies could be naked and uncovered without catching chill. Even Arthur stopped his wanderings once the weather turned cold, though his presence made our marriage bed as lively as an empty flour sack. Arthur did not dress in front of me and he woke after me, his back turned as I dressed; he would wash in the pond with the hired men at day's end. There were no airs or better examples for my husband; Maude glared as she watched him splash alongside the ducks and field hands, and then stomped about whenever I came into view, as if I had been the one pushing him to behave as such.

One evening as I ironed his shirts, Arthur paused behind me in such a way that I feared his husbandly affection was at long last ripening.

"Good evening, sir," I said, not wanting to be rude.

"You press that toward no profit," he said. "The cuffs are twice darned and the buttonhole ripped. Give it to the serving girl to use for rags," he added.

"But surely one of your men could use it?"

"If you like," he said. "But I'll not go about as such. You must attend well to what I say, wife. Keep your pride about yourself and the custom we present to others."

I thought of him, washing beside the squawking fowl in the mud. "I have a fine hand for stitches, sir. But I am not skilled in sewing clothing."

"Neither is my sister," he replied. "But you do not see her going about trailing ragged threads." He shook his head, tossed back more whiskey from the cup he'd had at dinner. "By God, but I forget you're a young one. Has nobody ever told you? Maude assumes far more than is proper."

He pulled the shirt from the board and tossed it on the floor. "This pressing—leave it for the serving girl. There are far more dignified pursuits than this for you, wife." I stared at the floor where the shirt, half-starched and once-neat, now lay in a heap, and thought of Mistress Hellerstadt's fruitless singing lessons. I could not imagine how to please both he and his sister in my actions.

"Now then. My man goes to town to buy what's necessary. Maude gives him a list. Have Maude add your bits and bobbins when she does. You can write, yes?"

I told him I could; I kept my face still though beneath it lay a storm. Of course, I could write—I had written our names in the Ganey Bible. That evening, I lay beside him, listening to the rumble of his breath while I totted up all the things I wanted and hoped for. The next evening after dinner I mentioned to Maude that I should like Arthur's man to fetch me some notions.

"I have already given Mr. Casey my list," she said.

Patrick, Patrick, whom I had not been able to see in the manner I was accustomed for two weeks. All those nights I'd lain beneath him, and I could have told him direct what I'd lacked. All that he did to my flesh, and I did to his; I had no inkling that he could serve another role.

"Go find him yourself should you want to add to it," Maude added.

This last came from her as a kind of dare; she doubted that the mousy girl-wife of her brother, who was fearful of asking for such feminine trifles, would push further to ask the frightful hired man.

But Patrick was not frightful to me. And given that he was back by the chicken run, talking and eating with the other laborers, telling him didn't even require stealth. He didn't write it down, just nodded, polite, and I whisked the other direction, feeling eyes on my back.

I picture this often. Turning on my heel, the young girl pretending at bravery, under the heavy evening sky. A small favor, small items. Small haughty gestures. Grief makes us so small, even in this place, where the fields go on like waves.

You should have asked for more, I think now, seeing my girl-self spin away from the man I loved more than anything. A crystal chandelier, a crate of oranges, a bolt of black satin or scarlet tulle.

Patrick left the following morning. It would be nearly a fortnight before he returned. His arrival was signaled only by the paper-wrapped packages left that afternoon on the back stairs. But inside them, no needles, no brown thread. Into further sadness I sunk. He had forgotten; my desires were not on Maude's list, and asking after them might mean she would scold him. I wished to scold him. It was everything, nothing—a package of needles, a spool of dun-colored thread—and I burned to ask him the reason he had not complied.

That night, Arthur lingered after supper. He drank whiskey with his coffee and spoke of wanting to buy the Haedesches' farm—its assets were many: an orchard, a pasture that rolled level and green, ideal for grazing, a small creek between the two larger fields. He would have to keep the family on-site, that was his wish, as a compassionate man. The elder Haedesch brother was in ill health, while the younger Haedesch was widowed with children. Maude did not reply beyond nodding. Her fingertips edged around the faded gilt of the good china we ate evening meals on, and beyond us in the kitchen we could hear the humming of the one of the girls Arthur benevolently thought of now, sweeping the floor, and no doubt eager to get to her own bed.

Once the plates were gone, however, Arthur remained. Whether it was the whiskey or the tin cup he drank it from that made Maude frown wasn't clear. She went to sew in the parlor while he remained at the table. I was unsure between them. I went into the kitchen, instead, dismissed the washing girl, who sprang out the back like a caged cat, leaving the dirty dishwater. The sky was dimming as the first stars came out. I had a cracked sole on my left boot and I hadn't run since childhood and I had no place to go, but I wanted to flee. These people did not care for me. I disappointed Maude; I confounded Arthur.

I tossed the fouled water, hung the bucket on its peg, and ran. Across the years, I can see how foolish I was. I was so young. That was my chief credential, though. My body was resilient. Fear of losing the last bit of light sent me straight to the only place that would have me. Where I could speak as I wished. Move as I desired. I was breathless. I surprised Patrick. I found that I liked surprising a man as he lay down for his evening's rest.

Chapter Eleven

The Isherwood house was eerie, the screen door open and the living room empty. When she knocked, Rusty barely lifted his head from the couch. Beer bottles and paper plates still dotted the side tables, and a program from the funeral with Evie Isherwood's face on it was tucked up on the mantel between vases of wilted flowers. All the windows were open, though the Isherwoods, like the Dunedins, had central air.

For a moment, she wanted to call out for Hugh. But then she was frozen with the idea that this didn't have to happen. Poppy wouldn't like any deviation from her orders, and here she was, detouring at Hugh's house, the sleeping bags she had promised to bring completely forgotten.

"Hello?" Hugh's voice, from the second floor.

She didn't answer, just skipped up the stairs, her shoes dusty from running down Old Blackmun Road. Sweat streamed down into her bra, settling into the waistband of her cutoff shorts. She had not worn underwear today—she had run out of clean ones after her period had ruined so many of them—and the bra was an old one of Lilah's, too small, with a pattern of little frogs hopping all over it. That Hugh would see this made her stop at his half-open bedroom door. That everyone else who lived these secrets had adjusted their routines accordingly—washed underwear, bought cute bras, planned ahead—made her feel weary and childish. That she had no one she could bring these questions to was also unbearably lonely. Gretel wouldn't be home for weeks. Would Daisy be ready to talk about these things with her by then?

She pushed open the door. Hugh sat on the edge of his bed, barefoot in just black basketball shorts. His chest looked red from too much sun and his face bunched up from crying.

Sitting beside him, she pressed her palm to his thigh. His room was unexpectedly tidy. The bed was made, the laptop on his desk was closed, the rug on the wood floor scored with vacuum marks. A pile of clothes in a hamper was the only mark of clutter. Beside her, she could feel him shaking. He apologized, dabbed his eyes with his knuckles.

"It's all right," she said. He lay in her lap, his breath at first soft and uneven on her thigh, then becoming sobs. She hadn't ever pictured someone seeking solace from her like this. She had seen his tears at his mother's funeral but that was like a prop, a costume. These were sounds she didn't tend to make herself. His mouth open, his nose sniffling, his voice gargling things that could have been words but didn't track as language.

Maybe words weren't possible when you felt this way. Maybe it was from not letting these feelings have their way with you, once and for all, from denying them entrance for so long. She stroked his shoulders, the flat of his jaw. What they had been doing these past few days was not romance. It was just a space of time between his mother's end and this moment, him spattering and babbling on a girl who couldn't help him in any real way besides being adjacent to another he had wanted. This she understood, as foul as it felt to recognize it. They were all that was clear and calculable, with a sum of nothing. A net with a hole, zero plus nil, a needle losing its thread. Sadness seeking sadness. It was a while before he stopped and looked at her.

"Sorry," he said. "My dad's at my brother's for the weekend. I didn't want to go. I couldn't."

"It's okay."

"It just, being around everybody and my aunts? They all look so much like her . . . I don't . . . I'm being such a pussy. It's stupid," he said.

She squeezed his thigh again. She liked that part of him. So sturdy and strong. When he turned toward her, she kissed him, her mind as clear as an iced-over lake.

Chapter Twelve

Later, as he placed a wrapped paper package on my dress, which he always took care to fold on his chair, he said, "I could kill him, if you like."

"What would that make you? Hush."

"Young missus tells me to hush." He was amused. "Already I have made myself whatever I am."

"You are not quite twenty," I said. I could hear the wind whine, wend its way through the cracks in the logs of his hut.

You deserve brick and stone, he later said. *Not any of this rubbish.*

Beneath him, my skin felt soft as warm leather. The straw tick poked my back and his blanket was coarser than any I'd ever slept on, here or back home, but no wind could slip between us. He was so warm.

"I don't understand, Jane," he said. "He does not lie with you?"

"Only once."

"He did not give you his fill?"

"Aye, he did. The once."

His face became rough. He turned on his side, his palm over my belly. My insides churned, still, though it had been at least an hour since we'd joined. The moon had risen beyond the small window toward the stable. What he had done to my body was the finest bit of magic. I loved to be touched so. Even after it was done, everything crackled and sparkled. But he had never given me his fill, himself. Always, he spent outside of me.

"Is he . . . was he harsh to you, Jane?"

I explained Arthur's gentleness, his caution. The basin he filled, the cloth he had placed beside it. The empty marriage bed nearly all the evenings since.

"He is not as a man should be, Jane," Patrick said. "You do not deserve such. This is not a husband."

"I presumed it was that I did not know how to be a proper wife."

He sighed, his mouth on my jaw. Silk and straw, softness and whiskers. "You are more than a proper wife. And even so, a lass does not learn what her master bids if he does not speak with her."

"He is not my master."

"There you are mistaken, my queen," he said sadly. "'Tis both our masters."

It was not quite dawn when I fled through the trees and across the fields to the Ganey house. I ran back with similar vigor, but none of the fear I'd carried out. Inside, the kitchen was still but for flies buzzing about the open butter crock. The table was stripped of its cloth. Only Arthur's empty whiskey cup remained. Maude's shawl hung on its peg, her snores from the end of the hall constant.

The open door to my room showed my bed as smooth as an icy lake. Nobody in this house might love me, but across the way, there was one man who cared if I lived. He had kissed my mouth like something holy, licked my breast, entered my body with contentment. He always laughed like a boy at play when it was done, his pride ringing through his tiny, mean hut.

Only for your fine hand, Jane. From this day forward. All I do will be for you.

In the parlor, movement startled me. Arthur, waking as he sat slumped in the chair by the fire. His face was obscured in the dim as the hesitant sun rose through the window. I expected him to rise, to shout, to strike me. To wake Maude. That last I feared the most.

But he merely stood, brushed the wrinkles from his trousers, and nodded, stepping around me toward the kitchen, and said not one word.

I undressed, carefully hanging my dress, brushing the burrs from the hems and sweeping them under the bed. In my shift, I went beneath the quilts and shivered. I could still smell Patrick's body, how he had anointed me, his queen. But now the scent of my husband lingered on the linens like it had never before, and fear unraveled through my limbs. As the first rooster crowed, I closed my eyes. In my hand, a wax package of needles and three spools of thread.

Chapter Thirteen

What she liked the most was that she didn't feel the need to speak. Probably this was wrong, in some way. Probably they should share things. Thoughts, dreams, courtesy questions— *What's your middle name? Your favorite color?*—but Daisy liked being only her body with Hugh. She liked how kissing him made his tears stop and his hands begin to move over all the parts of herself she had only considered in mundane, familiar ways. He smelled her neck and licked it. He laid her back on his tidy bed and slowly pushed up her shirt, kissing her shoulders, brushing his fingers over her breasts. He made sounds in his throat that made her lower belly twist and pull. He didn't ask where her sisters were or what time she needed to go home or whether she minded if he unclasped her frog bra and took it off. Between all of these actions, he returned to kiss her, his tongue insistent on hers, small pauses where she might have stopped him. Said something.

But she wanted to do neither. It made her want to laugh, lying on this bed that smelled like pine needles and the clinically scented soap found in school lavatories, his body athletic, alive with pur-pose. When he unbuttoned her shorts, she could see his hard dick beneath his own, sticking up slightly to the right. He smiled at see-ing her completely bare, tossed her shorts on the floor, and stood to step out of his own. Then he came over to her, his naked body as sticky and warm as hers. The breeze from his open window did nothing to cool them. When he lifted his mouth from hers, she smiled, and touched his jaw.

"Are you afraid or anything?" he asked. "Do you feel okay?"

"Yes."

Lower, still. Her mind went wild with words she would not say: *pubes, maiden hair, Pussy, vagina, Cunt.*

He kissed down her body. Belly button, the curve beneath that.

His mouth there didn't make her body revolt; it felt soft and quiet. But then he wrapped his hands around her hips tighter, like he was trying to make a point. She stared at the ceiling fan, trying not to frown, feeling tense in equal measures to his enthusiasm. She hoped her period was really over. Poppy said that by the time the blood started becoming lighter brown, it was basically ending. None of this appeared to be on his mind. His hands spread her thighs wider.

She shut her eyes. If she thought of herself as a body only! Not Daisy, not Poppy's cousin, not a girl in a boy's room, a place she shouldn't be, doing what she shouldn't be doing. *Just a body. Only that.*

And then, a kind of rhythm began. He had made it, or she had—did it matter who? She stretched toward the headboard and pressed back, acknowledging the beat. His fingers went inside her, like the day of his mother's funeral, a breach that made her shiver. She knew this feeling from the dream of the faceless woman, and she knew what would happen if he did not stop. She wanted to say something but could not figure how to phrase it. But soon it was clear he knew, too, because he whispered, "Daisy, Daisy, yes."

When it happened, her back curved off the bed, her mouth wanting to shout but only gasping. He lifted up, grinning, his fingers sliding out from her. He looked down at his hand, which was glittering and slick.

"No blood," he said. She felt a twang of shame. She could see him now, fully hard. The last light of the sunset made both of their skin as livid as meat. He bent down and kissed her.

"Do you want to?"

"Okay," she said. She shut her eyes, listened. Waited. The mattress sank unevenly, a drawer opened. Sweaty hands tearing plastic. She opened her eyes; he was concentrating on unrolling the condom down his penis. *I am just my body*, she thought, eyes closing again, sighing at the feeling of his skin on hers.

Chapter Fourteen

I had not known it while I was his wife, but Arthur had always known what he was. In my death, I came to know all of him, long after it might have been of use.

For himself, there was no ill will toward me. What a blessing to learn! He was merely a man as any other. The lines between male and female were clear to him. Here, he would wash in the pond with the hired men; there his sister would direct the serving girl and the timing of lunches, teas. His mother, before her death, was a great ship steering the family toward fresh linens, soft lamplight, gifts wrapped in brown paper and string. His father always covered in dust, always beating his hat against his thigh, his mouth like the string on the brown-papered gifts, tight and silent.

Toward the notion of marriage he had never struggled. He understood that it was as necessary as anything else in life: a horse fence, a protected well, the long days during harvest. He saw it as less than a conquest, but a bit more than a transaction. A man hauled in a woman like a fish in a net; the woman pushed out your children, who would grow up to do the same. His own parents hadn't fought this expectation, though they did not seem to delight in it. To fulfill that role was like any other task of pulling life out of the dark earth. A task you did and did not question.

All of this remained scored on his mind like any other certainty when he went deer hunting with the younger Haedesch brother, Paul: the delight of sunrise, the irritation of mosquitoes at dusk. Months had passed since Haedesch had buried his wife after she had loosed their fourth living child, another daughter, and gone to her own final rest. Autumn was coming and there had been a sickness in Haedesches' pigs; the family required meat for the winter to come.

Arthur did not like Haedesch, but he had not disliked him, either. They were neighbors. He attended his wedding, sent over ale after the births of his children. The party he attended had been a fine one in his memory. I would have enjoyed it, had I been.

Finer in Arthur's memory was the hunting. After they had shot two deer and split open the bodies to dress them for the journey home, Paul removed his boots and shirt and bent to wash in the shaded spring that ran between two fields. The wedding ring on his hand still winked gold in the midday light. Arthur joined his neighbor, opening a pack of food his sister had sent with them. Haedesch nodded, accepted the bread and meat and fruit preserves. They ate in the cool of the stream and the trees, listening as crows screamed above them. Afterward, his neighbor shared a jug of sweet wine, the color of light on water, and then he slapped his hand against Arthur's thigh, squeezing. They stared at each other, and then Haedesch murmured in German and unbuttoned his own trousers. Hand on himself, Haedesch leaned back, smile on his face dappled by the sun. Not wanting to appear unsporting, Arthur released himself similarly, though he left on his boots. Together, they were silent, smiling, glancing at the other at times, while they each pressed toward release. When Haedesch finished, he grimaced and fell back against the grass, gasping as if he'd just entered cold water. Arthur followed him. Then Haedesch laughed, raising his palm toward Arthur in a kind of praise, the pale liquid sliding between the third and pinky fingers where his wedding band remained tight.

"You are a good hunter, Arthur," Haedesch said, squatting to wash in the creek. He whipped palmfuls over his face, his chest, beneath his arms. "You will come again with me after the women divide up the meat?" His words laced with Teutonic lilt, candor, Arthur said he would.

"I will bleed them in the forest beyond the orchard," Haedesch said. "There is a dry house, like such." He raised his hands, indicating height. "No wolves will find what we bring there."

Arthur told him he knew the place, had gone there as a boy when his father was still alive. "Your father built it, Haedesch, when I was a lad," he said.

"You will call me Paul, neighbor," he said. "We shall have only our Christian names between us."

✦

✦

✦

When he returned home later in the afternoon, he startled his sister, naked and washing, her foot curved over the hip bath as she scrubbed between her toes. He admired her body, which he had known since he could remember. She was as tall and broad as he, her hair dark gold when damp, her muscles thick and splendid. She had not been given his fine features, which their mother called a curse. In this memory, which I cannot shake, which I strangely treasure, as it was the closest I felt to Maude as a sister, or friend, I found her beautiful. It makes me angry, thinking of her in the bath, an unflinching nude Boudica, earning her brother's apology.

"I am sorry, Maude," he said.

"Write your letters," she said, intent on the rough skin of her heel and ankle. "I will not ask again."

He nodded. He was ashamed. He wrote the letters while he ate a bowl of stew, then joined his men in sawing joists for the barn. He slept through a thunderstorm, his body heavy and sated. The next morning, he met with Paul in the place beyond the orchard. The hut was open to the sky to allow a fire and great sinister hooks lurked in the ceiling. Old blood darkened the floor but there were no carcasses.

"I have arrangements," Paul said, a wave of his hand. He passed him a twist of apple leather, a jug of water. He sat down, gestured for Arthur to do the same. They sat against the wall, eating and drinking. Paul said his hired man needed the meat for a journey; they must hunt again in the morning.

Arthur asked where his man was going.

"To bring me a new bride," Paul said. "I am all daughters."

Arthur nodded, thinking of his letters.

"We shall go before first light," Paul said, slapping Arthur's knee, and rising. "Beyond here is a good place. Down by the water the animals like to drink."

Arthur agreed. He knew of the place.

"Return here this night," Paul said, shaking out his hat. "I will bring a blanket and make a fire. It is not so cold, together in this house. With a fire, it is a castle." He laughed.

That evening, all was as Paul had promised. Wool blankets in a nest, the fire low but hot in the center where the blood had dripped. Paul wore no shirt as he cleaned his rifle. He passed Arthur a bottle of the same golden wine. Arthur dropped his pack in the corner. Removed his own shirt. He had already cleaned his rifle, but he did the ritual again, a mirror of the man across from him.

Paul talked of the girl who was coming to marry him, once the minister came round next. He talked of his daughters, who he thought beautiful and strong. The youngest had a singing voice that gave him especial pride. The fire died, but they did not feed it. Paul removed his trousers, tipped his head at Arthur, who did the same.

"Come, neighbor," he said. "The fire is warmer beside me."

This night was the standard of every night, sharing what they'd shared at the creek, with mouths on mouths, hands twisting across each other, groans, shudders, Paul laughing as he spilled onto Arthur's neck.

Even when there was no hunting to be done, Arthur ended each night at the place beyond the orchard, always bringing his rifle. Paul warned of wolves and coyotes, though Arthur saw naught but raccoons and sprinting deer. He waited on the wool blankets, sometimes building his own fire, sometimes sweating without moving. Sometimes Paul arrived. Sometimes he did not. By the time the first winter came, Arthur found he could not sleep well anywhere besides this place. Even when Paul could not join him— his daughters caught a fever, a sow farrowing—Arthur rested contentedly, the memory of Paul's eyes glittering above the embers as they touched each other with joy and desperation always with him.

Chapter Fifteen

She had assumed Poppy would text or call. But her phone remained quiet as afternoon turned to evening, through Hugh getting her a glass of juice, through more touching and kissing as the first booms and cracks of fireworks exploded in the distance. Through a shower he invited her to share, where she learned how strange it was to wash one's hair and body with an audience. Through toweling dry and failing to dress, her clothes on the floor too wilted to put on fresh skin.

"I need to get back," she said. He was coiled around her in his bed, his mouth at her shoulder.

"I'll walk you home."

"You don't have to."

"Is Poppy home?"

"No."

"Then what's the big deal?"

"She's at Wade's with Lilah. I have to go back over there. I was supposed to . . . She wanted me to bring our sleeping bags and . . ."

"What?"

"We're . . . It's like a campout?"

"At Wade's?"

"Well, kind of."

"Poppy . . . and Wade? Hanging out?"

"Lilah, too." She sat up, her hands over her chest, and looked at the floor scattered with their clothes. One shirt, two pairs of shorts, and Lilah's old bra. All that kept them apart. She hated that Poppy might have been here, too, in this bed, Hugh's hands on her, Hugh's clothes beside hers. She picked up her shorts and pulled them on.

"Daisy, what's wrong?"

Nothing was wrong. Everything was good. As long as she stayed here in his room, and he didn't mention Poppy or ask any more questions, it would be okay.

He turned toward her. "Seriously, Poppy can't stand Wade. And I know he thinks Lilah's cute and all. But . . ."

He watched as she fastened Lilah's frog bra around her waist and pulled it up over her chest. "I can't tell you," she said. "It's not . . . I wasn't supposed to come here. Or say anything. And it's all going to be fine. Probably." She put on her shirt. He was still sitting on the bed under the quilt, the top of his dick hair fanning out. They'd gotten beneath the covers after the shower, when the night air had cooled everything down.

"Just tell me what's going on," he said. "You don't have to go anywhere. And I won't tell anyone. I swear."

Never before in her life did she want something so much as to stay here, to not have a family, to not have sisters who pulled her in so many directions. She looked at the ceiling, where the fan spun low and lazy, and considered all that freighted down getting her wish.

"We had to go somewhere else," she said. "Somewhere that my mom and aunt wouldn't be around."

"Is this about the tree?"

"No."

"Because my dad's insurance will pay for it," he said. "It's not a big thing, I mean, except for the hole in the roof and all that. But that house is old and . . ."

"It's not about the tree," she said.

"Then, is it Poppy? Because, Jesus. She's still pissed, after a year?"

"She said you sent her a dick pic," Daisy said. "Not asked her to marry you."

He got up and put on his shorts. He stood in front of her, hands in his hair, then on his hips. She liked how his body looked, even sunburnt. Even the hairs around his belly button, several shades darker than that on his head. Even right now, when they were talking about Poppy. She hated that she liked looking at him so much.

"I don't know what that has to do with anything," he said. "But I fucking asked her. And she said no. She fucking laughed, okay? Said no and laughed. I didn't send her shit. She and I? We never even . . . We didn't even do it, all right?"

"You expect me to believe that?"

"Well, it's the truth," he said. "Ask her yourself. She didn't want to do shit besides kiss and whatever." That he sounded peeved about this made Daisy flinch.

"Why would you ask her to marry you, then?"

"I don't know. I just wanted to. I wasn't thinking too clearly at the time, all right?"

"Do you still want to."

"No," he said. "Not really. I mean, I really liked her. I've always liked her, Daisy. I was always trying to keep up with her. It was like once middle school was over, she didn't give a shit about me."

"But you were always going out with some other girl," Daisy said. "What did you expect, for her to chase after you? Poppy would never do that."

"Right," Hugh said. "And that's what was cool about her. I guess. But, I figured, we've grown up here, we hung out since we were little kids. And she knows my mom. Knew her, I mean. It all made sense. We didn't know, then, that it wouldn't ever work."

Daisy nodded. She had no idea if he was referring to his mother surviving or Poppy marrying him.

Her phone beeped in the pocket of her shorts, and he stepped close to her to see who it was.

"Speak of the devil," he said.

"I gotta go get the sleeping bags," she said. "Shit."

He took her hand. "Will you just tell me what's going on? Please?"

She looked directly into his eyes. Blue and watery, his eyelashes darker than his hair.

◆

◆

◆

"I don't understand," he said. "Why don't you just ask someone for the money?"

"Who would we ask?"

He shook his head, shrugged. The road was dark except for the one light at the corner by the Isherwoods' mailbox. Around them the night hummed with crickets and the booms of fireworks. Occasionally, a few streams of light shot up and then thudded in the distance.

"Can't your aunt . . . Isn't she able to do that stuff?"

"No," Daisy said.

"But isn't it just, like, pills you take now?"

"Yes, but she didn't want to take them. I think Poppy made her, but I don't know. They just went into the bathroom and closed the door. She wouldn't even take pills for her depression. She doesn't like things that aren't natural."

"Like condoms, for instance."

"Ha, funny,"

"Who's the fuckin' dad, then?" he asked. "Does she know?"

"Tyler Haytch."

"Fucking Jesus," he said. "That dickweed?"

"He's just one possibility. There's a lot of guys who could be. She won't say."

"Fucking Tyler Haytch." Hugh shook his head. "Can't ask that prick to piss on you if you were on fire."

"She doesn't want him to know anything about it," Daisy said.

"Smart. He'd probably call the fuckin' cops, knowing him. But . . . what if something goes wrong?" he asked.

"I guess . . . we go to the hospital," Daisy said.

"Maybe you should just tell your mom?"

"She doesn't want to."

"I get that, but it's kinda something your mom oughta know, don't you think?"

"Hugh," she said, saying his name for the first time to him, feeling how it was like Poppy had said—just a puff of air, nothing at all. "Nobody is going to do anything unless my sister says so. I can't . . . You don't get it. No one ever listens to what I think."

"But you have to tell them! Or, fuck, just tell your mom yourself," he said.

"I can't. If it doesn't work, Poppy will deal with it."

"But Lilah's your fuckin' sister! Poppy's only your cousin!"

"She might as well be my sister," Daisy said. "I've lived with her all my life. I can't remember a time when she wasn't my sister. When they told me she was technically my cousin, I didn't believe them at first."

"When did they tell you?"

"Second grade."

He turned this over, his face contemplative. "I'd have given you the money," he said. "I'd have done it. If you'd asked, I would have. I still can."

"It's not just the money, we'd need gas and a car," Daisy said. "And if it got really late, who knows when we'd get home, and how we'd explain that?"

"Shit," he said. "All of that—we could have thought of something."

"It's not even your problem, Hugh," she said. "Poppy is going to be so mad at me for telling you."

"Yeah, well." He kicked gravel. "That's her being stupid. When someone offers help, you take it. Because people gotta help people. They just do."

They turned toward her driveway. She wanted to tell him that he was naïve. People helped other people when they could, because they had enough, and then some more to give. But she knew he wouldn't agree, and the truth was that none of what Lilah had done should involve Hugh or Wade. But here they were, both putting themselves into the middle of it. A firework screeched in the air, impossibly long, and the front step light flared to life.

"Shit," Hugh said, and nudged her off the driveway, toward the stand of trees, the brush scraping up her legs.

She looked closer and saw Mr. Isherwood's red truck—Hugh's red truck—in the driveway. And Mr. Isherwood standing on the stoop of her house, staring up at the motion light and the giant fallen maple looming above his head like a bridge in the night.

"Hugh, stop . . ."

But he kept on, pulling her farther into the brush. A branch smacked her face, and she hissed more from panic than pain. Any protest would just be more noise.

He stopped just short of the Ruin, crouching low behind a toppled tree. Daisy had found a nest in this tree last summer, a curated curved bowl of sticks and shreds of water-logged paper. She never figured out what kind of creature had occupied it. Hugh was staring at his father, who was turning at different angles to look at the tree that had punctured his property. But he didn't seem upset. The look on his face was more of marveling wonder than concern. He fidgeted, brushing something against his thigh. A bouquet: pink coneflowers, red beebalm, yellow black-eyed Susans.

"What . . . ," she started to ask Hugh, but his face was fixed, vacant.

Headlights poked through the trees; a car trudged up the road, turning onto the driveway slowly, until Daisy could hear the murmur of news on the radio. Carna.

"Shit," Daisy said. Hugh said nothing.

They watched as Carna got out of the car and Mr. Isherwood walked toward her, his steps slow but confident. They exchanged words, but nothing Daisy could make out. Carna pulled her suitcase and bag out of the back seat, and Mr. Isherwood offered to take the load. Then she saw the flowers, and they stood looking at each other.

Mr. Isherwood said something, and the flowers in his hand tilted to the side. Carna dropped her things and her head hung in defeat or exhaustion, Daisy couldn't tell which. Mr. Isherwood walked toward her, put his arms around her, the flowers pressed to her back. When she lifted up her head, he bent to kiss her, and for the first time in her life, Daisy saw Carna touch someone that way. She had never even seen her own mother kiss anyone like that: mouths aslant, arms reaching, hands pulling down. They were still kissing when Hugh swore and took off without caution, noisy as a buck in rut, through the brush toward Wade's house.

Chapter Sixteen

Patrick knew that I was increasing before I told him. This frightened me. If he, a boy just twenty, knew my secret all the way across the field, far from where I cast up my accounts nearly every morning and struggled to tie my skirts in the usual way, how did Maude not see?

But he said there was a fullness in my face that told him the entire tale.

"The way your skin smells, your hair is brighter, too." His mouth murmured against my neck. He was all pride where I was seized with fear.

"Does withdrawing not suit, after all?" I whispered. We only had a small time tonight; Arthur was expected back by sunset. He had gone to sell cattle with Mr. Haedesch.

"Perhaps not," he said. "I've never had a lass under me as long as you, Jane."

This displeased me. For I was under him, sure as he spoke. And I did not want to think of others in my stead, in the past or the future. What lay between us, what we had made tonight in darkness and stealth, was difficult enough. Though something lived within me, threatening to grow still further as the weeks let on, I had never felt smaller. I said as much to Patrick, and he, never being slight by his own admission, tried for consolation.

"Fine goods come tied in small parcels," he said. "And untied . . ."

"Stop. We cannot. I must get back. What shall we do? I do not want to stay here, Patrick. I do not want to have his child."

"'Tis not his."

"'Twill be," I said. "This is why come Maude sent for Bess and me."

"I shouldn't like to be Maude," he said. "Sending for girls who can never prosper under her brother's attentions."

Patrick was dark on this subject. He considered Arthur as if he were no more significant than a blown spiderweb, when the man provided him both wage and whack.

I told him of the woman Maude and her callers discussed, who lived alongside the river. "The witch of the woods, a hag from a granny's tale," Maude said, and laughed.

"I could visit her, had I coin," I said.

"Nay," he said. "You think us between muck and nettles, but there are other means of escape. Maude has a tongue that could clip a hedge, but you appraise her short if you think she hasn't designed this entire affair. She knows what we have made. She has wished for it herself."

"How?"

"She knows what her brother is. Better than all of the county's whispers, she knows himself all too well," Patrick said. "She knows that should he die, and have no heir, she'll be pulling the devil by the tail to shake out a living from these lands. No doubt she meant for one with less hairy heels than myself to do this job for her, but she meant for something in your belly or your sister's. And she knew Ganey can't put it there seeing as he's selling cattle with Haedesch all the days of his life."

"You are wicked," I said, "Or do you speak plain?"

"Plain as the puddle in the road," he said, "But you and your sister were not the first to be caught in her tangle. You remember the school rhyme: 'Twas you and your sister. One of the old housemaids heard both Ganey and his sister squawking about it one night while she was sweeping up; she told a lad she was sweet on, who told one of the field hands. Maude Ganey has tried to account for her brother's condition twice before. Both lasses run off. By the hole in my coat, I'd wager that Bible of theirs has been blotted and smudged long before I pulled you from the water."

"Then she means me no shame," I said.

"Aye," he said. "But you're no more than any other animal she owns. And that is what I can't allow. You must go, soon, I know it. But hear this, sweet lass. I want you more than any other thing beneath the sun and stars. I want you, and I want what you carry beneath your belly. That is my child, and I'll not turn it over to a high-handed nag, her cleverness be damned."

"What shall we do, then?"

"It is my lot," he said. "I gave you this green gown, but I shall make it whitened in good time, do not doubt it. You must keep your head about you."

"I cannot keep my breakfast about me."

"Fill your belly with bits all day as you go; you will feel less faint. Leave the scheme to me."

"How may you conspire on your own?"

"I am thinking long to being more of a comfort to you. But we shall outsmart Maude Ganey. And I present to you all I have got, box and dice. Do you accept? Will you have me?"

"As a husband? By rights, I cannot."

"The page in a Bible is not for us," he said. "Live in my heart, and pay no rent, Jane Murphy. That will be all the oath I require."

Chapter Seventeen

From the back of Wade's house, she could see the light of the enormous television and hear snapping and popping, low voices. Across the field a fire was dying between two men who slouched in lawn chairs. Daisy veered toward the patio, where Wade was drinking a beer at the picnic table and Hugh was on the back step, lighting off Black Cats, a pinch of chew rounding out his lower lip. Dead firecrackers scattered across the concrete patio.

"Hey," Wade said.

Hugh said nothing. He spit a bit of tobacco but didn't look at her.

"Are my sisters inside?" she asked.

"Yup," Wade said. "Watching that same show."

"*The Reavers*," Hugh said, miserably lighting matches and tossing them at his feet. "All girls love that shit."

"Is that why you're out here?" Daisy said, trying to sound casual. Hugh's indifference made her skin feel like breaking glass. "Can't handle season two?"

"Season two's fine with me," Wade said. "That girl can bang her brother as long as she takes off her shirt. What do I care? Ha!"

Hugh glanced at Wade and then back to the box of Black Cats.

"Poppy doesn't want Hugh anywhere inside the house," Wade said. "So we took the party outside."

"Not even her goddamn house," Hugh grumbled. Daisy sat down on the picnic bench. She was feeling dizzy.

"She's pretty pissed," Wade said.

Daisy shrugged. "Nothing new there."

"No, more than usual," Wade said. "And especially at you."

"Is Lilah okay?"

"She's been pretty sick the last hour," Wade said. "In the bathroom. You know. But she doesn't even complain."

Daisy wanted to ask what was happening in the bathroom. Blood? Vomit? Shit? She couldn't think of a way to say it that wouldn't embarrass Lilah or enrage Poppy. She could hear, faintly, the rumbling orchestral title track of *The Reavers*. "My aunt's home," she said.

"I know," Wade said. Then he sat across from her at the picnic table and set down his beer. "That's one reason Poppy won't let him in the house." He nodded toward Hugh.

"You *told* her?" Daisy asked him.

"Of course I fucking told her," Hugh said. He still wouldn't look at her. "I thought she might already know."

"If she knew, why would she fucking go out with you?" Wade asked. "I mean, it's Poppy. Jesus. Do the math."

Hugh just kept lighting matches. "Whole family of fuckin'

liars," he said. "Fucking sitting there, living on my family's property, letting it go to shit, letting him pay for every goddamn thing. And the whole time, it's because what? Your fucking aunt can't figure out how biology works. Some goddamn midwife she is."

"You're being a prick," Wade said.

Carna had still been in nursing school when Poppy was born, Daisy wanted to say. But she knew how feeble that would sound.

"Fuck you, okay?" Hugh said. "Poppy's our age. Do the math yourself, dickhead."

Wade sighed. Drank his beer. "Funnest Fourth of July on record, huh?"

Daisy stood up and pushed past Hugh. "We're not a whole family of fuckin' liars," she said, moving toward the sliding glass door.

"It's locked," Wade warned.

"Well, you might as well be," Hugh said. "Seems like stupid runs in the family." Finally, he looked at her, his head tipping toward where Lilah and Poppy were sealed inside.

Tears came, instantly, like a summer storm, and she couldn't do anything to stop them. She remembered closing her eyes while he put on the condom and was flooded with shame. She banged on the glass, yelling, "Open up! It's me!" But nobody came; the TV was ragingly loud.

"You wanna be all mad, Isherwood, you might as well put it toward the fucker who did it," Wade said, his voice softer.

"My dad?" Hugh asked.

"No, Tyler Haytch," Wade said. "What, are you gonna go punch out your dad?"

"My mom just fucking died, Wade," he said. "She's dead, and this whole time . . . Now you want to go kick ass on Tyler Haytch? That sounds like a solid idea to you right now?"

Wade crushed the can in his fist. "Why the fuck not? Kid's had it coming for years."

Daisy wiped her tears, but her body kept shaking. "We don't know who it is. Who *cares* who it is. Just drop it. Stop finding reasons to be mad at everyone."

"Daisy, come on," Hugh said. His hand reached up to tug at her shorts. "Just . . . don't. I'm not mad at you."

"Sure seems like it," Wade said.

"Jesus! Give me a fuckin' break already! Sorry I'm not handling this shit in the perfect, best way, all right? Fuck."

"You're only guessing," Wade said. "You have no proof it's what you think."

Hugh shook his head. "It's gotta be. I've known for a while that you guys pay no rent on that place. When Brian went to college, all the financial shit had to be gone over and my mom found out about it and they had this big-ass fight."

"So, you think she knew, then?" Wade said. "That's what you're saying?"

"No, she was just wondering why my dad wasn't gonna collect income on property that technically belonged to her family," Hugh said. "And my dad said it was going to be counted as a loss and that, at first, Carna paid the utilities and whatever but things got hard when you all—"he waved toward Daisy—"moved in, so he just paid the utilities, too. It wasn't that big of a deal. My mom wasn't mad about it; she just wanted to start the strawberry patch and my dad was dragging his feet on it, saying cash was a problem. Then it comes out, he's not actually getting income where he could be. My mom felt sorry for you guys, Daisy. She accepted it. She really did. Because she was a fucking great person, okay?" He spit more dip on the patio, wiped his mouth. He looked miserable.

"She was," Wade said. "So maybe that's all there is to it. Why's it gotta be that they had some affair and a baby and shit?"

"No," Hugh said. "If there wasn't more to it, why would they be smacking it up in the goddamn driveway a minute after my mom died? Like, days after we scattered her ashes? That fucker. What the fuck."

Daisy sat down beside him on the step. "I hate this," she said. "I hate everything." Then she started crying again.

Now Hugh was kinder. His hand went around her back. "You didn't know. It's not like you could do anything. You're just a kid."

This was worse than his anger. The whiplash of her feelings was exhausting. She tried to breathe slower to calm herself. Violet was always exhorting them to "slow down, breathe" especially when Lilah became upset.

"You asked Poppy to *marry you*," Daisy said. "*You* did that." Wade laughed. "Dude!"

"I know!" Hugh said. He stopped touching her back and held his head in his hands. "You know how fucking gross that is?"

"You guys could be an episode of *The Reavers*," Wade laughed.

"Don't be a dick," Hugh said. "You know we never . . . Ah, fucking shut up, Dunedin."

"Too soon, too soon," Wade conceded.

"I was a fucking idiot," Hugh said. "I thought she and I would be perfect."

Daisy stood up. She couldn't be near him. It wouldn't have been perfect. It would have been exactly the same thing as before. Lies. Secrets. People wanting what they can't have. She recalled Mr. Isherwood sitting on Carna's porch, the whiskey and the paperwork between them. Her aunt's years of living across the road from the father of her child. Watching another family live and prosper while she scraped by with her clueless sister and two extra kids she didn't expect. All of them, Evie Isherwood included, watching their kids swim in the duck pond and roast marshmallows and celebrate birthdays, for years. This is what Hugh wanted? For everything to be recycled, like the chorus of a song? Like his mother's ashes turned into corn, soybeans, the wildflowers his father had brought to Carna?

Behind her, the door slid open, making her stumble.

Poppy. "We're having a problem, Wade," she said. "Can you take us into town?"

✦

✦

✦

Hugh drove, because Wade had been drinking. They took Mr. Dunedin's big Suburban so Lilah could have room to lie down.

"Do you have any cars that aren't humungous?" Lilah asked Wade, as he carried her out to the car and lifted her into the middle seat.

"Go big or go home," Wade said. But when he tried to lay her on her back, Lilah refused. "I'm okay. It feels worse when I'm on my back. Sorry for being such a Picky Vicky." She tried to buckle her seat belt but Wade told her it didn't work. He sat beside her and motioned for Daisy to climb in the other side. Hugh was starting the car, adjusting the seat so Wade had enough room behind him. Poppy rode in the front, directing Hugh where to detour from construction in Hogestyn, her voice calm as if there was no emergency. Like they were going to get an ice cream cone. Hugh did as she asked, steering the giant car carefully, and slower than Daisy guessed he'd normally drive.

Halfway to town, Lilah threw up in a plastic Walgreens bag. Wade wiped her mouth with his T-shirt and threw the bag out the window. All along the highway they could hear fireworks popping off. Lilah was joking that everything was too explosive today.

"You're just a Yakky Jackie," Poppy said, reaching across the back seat to hold her hand. Daisy noted that Hugh sped up just the slightest bit. His eyes found hers in the rearview mirror, and she looked away.

They were almost to the McDonald's before the turnoff to the hospital when Lilah said she needed to go to the bathroom.

"Now?" Poppy asked.

"Now."

Hugh didn't have to be told. He cranked the Suburban two lanes over and pulled up to the nearest door. Daisy jumped out, Lilah followed her, and Poppy told the guys to wait in the car.

"Get her a cup of water, will you?" Poppy told Daisy, before hustling Lilah to the restroom.

Daisy felt shy about asking for something when it was clear they weren't going to be customers, but the girl working the counter was sluggishly wiping down the register and didn't have anything else to do. Everyone was at the fireworks; later, the place might get slammed with hungry little kids and drunk teenagers. It was only nine thirty. It seemed so much later.

The bathroom smelled like the kind of chemicals that Lilah hated. She always chastised Carna for using bleach, saying lemon oil and white vinegar were just as good. Daisy waited, listening to the soft words on the other side of the stall.

"Feel like anything else is in there?" Poppy asked softly.

"I don't know."

"What all did you eat today?"

"A banana and some crackers. And pizza."

"So that's . . . You think that's it?"

"How should I know? I can't . . . There's nothing else. The cramps are bad. But I can't make anything else come out, Poppy. What do you want?"

"Well, how do you feel?"

"Thirsty. Tired. Gross. Can we just go home?"

Poppy came out of the stall and refused the water when Daisy offered it up. "I don't want her to touch anything in here."

"What's happening?"

"We're going home. It's starting. We can't take her anywhere now." Poppy washed her hands, staring at herself in the mirror. She pushed on the hand dryer and the screaming sound filled the bathroom. An old woman nudged into the restroom with a walker and they both went quiet. The toilet flushed and Lilah stepped out.

"It's not a lot of blood," she said. "Well, not as much as I thought."

"Shh," Poppy said, pointing to the other stall.

"Jesus, who cares?" Lilah said, washing her hands and then drying them by squeezing bunches of her hair. Blood vessels under her eyes had burst, giving her a demonic look. Daisy stepped aside and followed her sisters out of the bathroom.

Wade was standing in the order area when they came out.

"Well?"

"We're going home," Poppy said.

"My house or yours?"

"Yours."

"Okay. Can I order some food quick? Hugh's hungry. You guys want anything?"

❖ ❖ ❖

To Daisy's surprise, Poppy started drinking beer and playing cards with Wade on the picnic table. She was even sneaking his fries, wiping them in smears of ketchup on the paper bag that he was using as a plate.

Lilah was asleep in Mr. Dunedin's bed, wearing a giant HOGE-STYN FOOTBALL T-shirt with her just-washed hair wrapped in an ugly brown towel, a smaller TV glinting silently across from her on the wall. Hugh had gone over to Wade's drunk uncle's tiny bonfire and was standing with the two men, all three of them indistinguishable in the dark apart from the faint light of their fire, waving hands, and drinking beer. After giving Lilah more tea and sending her to the shower, Poppy explained to Wade and Daisy that it would be slowly happening now, the lining shedding in layers of blood and tissue onto the giant maxi pads they'd bought yesterday. Yesterday! It felt millions of years away. Now it was after midnight and Daisy sat on the sofa in front of the turned-off television, unable to calm down.

Her mind roiled with memories of her aunt and the mysterious genesis of Poppy, all the questions that had gone unanswered. As Daisy replayed trivial family stories she'd heard her whole life, the facts added up: Carna moving to Hogestyn in the middle of nursing school to help Grandma Whitsun pack up her house after she went into assisted living; Poppy being born, same year as Hugh; moving into the house on Old Blackmun Road when Grandma Whitsun's house sold. Then Poppy and nursing school and Violet's tales of the return from California. Carna had attended Daisy's birth as Violet's doula, which had kicked off her interest in obstetrics. Poppy and Hugh, swimming alongside each other in the Isherwoods' duck pond, the same blond hair, the same winning good looks. Why would it be a shock, aside from how well concealed the secret had remained? Evie Isherwood had always included the Whitsuns in everything; they were a cohort of young mothers, banding together to share the daily tasks of raising young children: walks in the woods; dips in the duck pond; meals of hot dogs and Popsicles. Everyone pitching in, soothing hurts, rocking sleepy heads, tossing each other's kids in the car for a quick run to town to offer a small bit of peace to the other women. If Evie Isherwood knew the truth, she was the most understanding wife in the world.

Wade and Poppy came inside, Wade burping and tossing empty beer cans into the sink. He waved good night and headed to his room, which was across the hall from his father's, a fact Daisy found adorable for some reason. Poppy used the bathroom and then came back out to stare at Daisy.

"What?"

"You're just sitting in the dark?"

"What do you want me to do?"

"Watch a show. Go to bed. Clean up the fucking kitchen."

"What if I don't want to do any of that?"

Poppy rolled her eyes, kicked off her sandals. "Why is it that one of you has to irritate the shit out of me at all times? Do you schedule it or something? Make sure every shift is covered?"

"But I'm not even doing anything!" Daisy shouted.

"Exactly," Poppy replied, pulling her hair out of its ponytail. "That's exactly the problem. Has been the whole time. Someday, Daisy, you're going to get what I mean. You're going to realize that you can't always be the baby of the family. Waiting for someone else to clean the mess and figure out what to do. I hope I'm around to see it, personally. It'll be a relief, actually."

Daisy crossed her arms over her chest. The house was too cold and there were no afghans or blankets anywhere she could see. Maybe men didn't care if they were cold. Maybe they didn't get cold. Maybe Mrs. Dunedin had taken all of them in the divorce.

"I'm going to bed," Poppy said.

"With Lilah?"

"Yes. Of course. Someone's got to be on top of things."

After she left, Daisy tried to watch television. But there were too many remotes and buttons and she couldn't do more than turn off the sound bar and make the video game console light up. She took off her bra and stuffed it under a cushion, then rummaged around looking for a blanket, finally discovering a Minnesota Twins fleece throw inside the giant footstool, which also housed a bag of Cheetos and a crumpled pack of cigarettes. She reclined on the sofa, waiting for sleep, needing it, but being unable to relax in this strange place. She hadn't slept in her own bed for the last week or so, which felt like the consequence for knowing what she knew, and doing what she had.

The facts of the day were too weird and held too much power. Daisy considered the possibility that nothing would go back into its proper order as it had been before. Poppy would leave again, and Lilah would deflate into torpor and the hole in the roof would flood and rot the walls and Violet would sing the praises of water, the blessing baptism it provided, the inevitability of change. Growth in death.

The sliding door shuddered; Hugh yanked it open, stumbling. Drunk. His hair was sticking up at all angles.

"Hey, where is everyone?"

"They're all asleep," Daisy said.

"Why? It's not even that late."

Daisy's phone was dead and she couldn't see any clocks nearby to dispute or verify this.

He blundered into the living room. "Can I sit by you?"

"Sure."

Slowly, he lowered himself and then kicked off his shoes, un-peeled his socks. He smelled sweaty and dirty, like beer and bonfire.

"Is your sister not-pregnant yet?"

"I don't know," Daisy said. "Poppy said the girl she knew who did the same thing, it took a couple of days."

"Jesus. I would never want to be a girl. No offense or anything," Lilah hasn't had a very good year," Daisy said. "Everything's been going wrong."

"Don't get why she thought Tyler Haytch would make it go right." Daisy didn't correct him. But she didn't know why Lilah did most things she did. Of course, Daisy had done things that also made no sense. She had gone to Hugh's today convinced it was the only option. Maybe you had to do things wrong before you could see the right way.

He leaned back, exhaled. "Fuck." His sweaty forearm spread over the throw that covered her calves.

"How's Wade's uncle?"

"He's a piece of work."

"Are he and his friend still drinking?"

"No, the friend went home; he has a riding lawn mower he drives around. So he'll probably get home around dawn. Jay's probably passed out by now. I pissed on his fire just to be safe but he wasn't too thrilled about that."

Daisy laughed. "He makes food on that thing, you know."

"Aw god, I know. So gross. Probably attracts raccoons. My piss is the least of it." His hand began rubbing Daisy on the leg, back and forth, through the fleece.

"Are you cold? There's probably another blanket in the foot-stool thing."

"No," he said, closing his eyes. His hand patted her legs now, haphazardly, like he was brushing something off. "No, I'm good, just like this. And so are you, Daisy. You're good. A really good kid. I won't ever tell anyone."

"Okay."

"Just don't feel bad about it," he said. "And you shouldn't, either. All right?"

"All right."

"Good night, Daisy."

"Good night."

He reached for the footstool, pulled it closer, then pulled the blanket off Daisy's legs a bit to cover his lap. She pulled up her feet, coiled on her side. His hand stretched out again, his fingers circling her ankle for a minute, then lying still spread over her bare calf. His skin felt warm, and gritty. Though her sisters were just a few feet away, she wanted him to want her again. The same things they'd shared in his bed hours earlier, in his shower. The ache this want produced in her chest was shameful and familiar. The same feeling she always had about being the youngest: a thing meant more to you than it did the older kids, who had grown up and moved past it. Didn't need it anymore. Didn't see why it was so important or necessary. She shut her eyes and willed herself to breathe, slowly. Not to cry. Just inhale and exhale, smelling Hugh Isherwood as his own breathing slowed to a regular hitched pattern, one that matched his unknowable dreams, in and out, until she recognized the logic of the faceless-woman dream overcoming her with the pull of its desires and fears, familiar and less frightening now, the same rhythm Wade kept, splayed across his comforter in his underwear, while the dreams of Poppy, just steps away, dark and ambitious in their own private cloud, swirled above as whatever lived inside in Lilah began its descent.

Chapter Eighteen

There is no time so fearsome as the days and weeks when one is with child. Cold nights put Arthur beside me in our bed, his great knobby knees and hitching snores crowding my calculations of Patrick's schemes. I counted my blessings—two dresses, three chemises, four caps, no coin—the child within was not amongst them. But the thought of his babe buoyed Patrick. I could hear his voice raised in joy as he called to the others in the morning. His proud voice was all I had of him as the cold and dark pressed down on us to winter. I dreamt of the woman by the river each morning when I woke and the creature inside me punched up, rejecting what I fed it.

One evening, as I stitched a second lining into one of my dresses, Maude stood in the light, her fist a knot on her hip.

"You have everything you require, Jane?"

"Pardon?"

"I asked—quite plain—if you should find yourself supplied

with all you need here. If we have given you that what will make you comfortable and keep you in good health?"

"Yes, ma'am. I find myself quite settled."

"Good," she said. "I should hope you might apprise me of anything that you might need. This winter is said to be much harsher than the last. It wouldn't do for you to be caught unawares."

"Yes, ma'am."

"I should like that you leave off your chores," she added. "It is best you leave the wash and such to Miss Haedesch as the weather turns."

"Oh, but I . . ."

"Mr. Ganey requires you to be of sound body and mind," she answered. "As do I. You may be young, but we cannot assume that will protect you forever. The cold that is coming . . . I wish for you peace and warm fires, Jane. I have put in orders for more cloth and thread. I should like to help you make ready for what's to come in spring."

✦
✦ ✦

Spring did not come for me. Only for my child. By Little Christmas, the day of my beloved's birth, I had not seen him for weeks. Ganey had errands for Patrick, sending him out in heavy snow and wind to collect rents and purchase sundries. I could not know of his schemes to escape, if they existed beyond his own mind. I was caught in Maude's parlor, stitching nappies and tiny collars, when I wasn't amending my own skirts to keep shape with my increasing belly. Arthur was about at all hours, hanging in doorways, commenting on the quality of the Maude's meals, inspecting his shirt buttons for loose threads. Winter pressed in, riming the windows and rattling the chimney, while I grew like a stuffed goose.

There were no smiles in such closeness. There was no laughter or song. I merely swelled like a tick and produced garments for a little Ganey child while Maude pondered what names might honor him appropriately. She was certain, by examining my carriage, that I would birth a boy, and often, while we sewed, she would list names, testing them in her voice: David, Malcolm, Angus.

"Our father's name was Hugo," she mused one day, and it was a physical strain to keep the particulars of my face in a proper expression.

In late February, the stove choked with wood and my body swollen to such heinous size that I could barely bend down to pick up a spool of thread, we received word from a visiting priest that Patrick had not arrived at the farmstead where he'd been sent to help shoe the horses. The master inquired through a series of messages when to expect him; had he been delayed by weather? The ice on the river was thick and there had been terrible winds. All travel was prohibited until spring.

Arthur had no means to inquire; we offered the priest a warm bed for the night. We had been shut up inside for a week after a blizzard had frozen the hens to their nesting and the snowdrifts reached to the middle of the parlor window. My fingers ached from stitching as though I'd been out in the white fields myself. I could not sleep, thinking of Patrick lost to that cold and ice. Arthur beside me did not improve this. Our feet and legs jostled for the wrapped bricks at the foot of the bed and I remained locked in shyness even when our bodies arranged in a truce and he took the dark and the quiet as opportunity to speak to me of his concerns. The weather, the barn's warmth, the woodpile shrinking, Maude's tempers. Never of the child I was to bear him. That was one topic he would not acknowledge, though he did take care to spread the quilt over me equally as we took our evening's rest and deliver me a cup of hot tea in the afternoon.

All I cared to have was news of Patrick, or of a break in the crushing cold. The furthest I could manage was a trip to the privy, which I had to make oftener than I'd like. Aside from the fussing of the priest, we had no callers and no way to call ourselves. One of the horses had gone lame in Patrick's absence, which Arthur groused about, though it had been his own fault for not hiring another man who knew animals.

When the weather broke a week after Lent, I rejoiced. I had no scheme—I was as great as Maude's china buffet—but the sun shining meant snow melting. No path could be made to anyplace beyond bed and privy. On a warmer evening when the snow dripped from the eaves in sorry plops, Arthur and Maude went to call on the Haedesch farm, to inquire about how they were keeping and to learn of any news. The door had not settled in its frame before I had my boots on, hardly laced for the reach of my belly, and a stocking of stolen coins tied to my skirts. My coat was heavy and the pattering of wet snow made it heavier still. I did not know where the woman on the river lived, but I knew the direction of it, had listened for it on lonely afternoons when I missed Bess and the sound of the waters of home in the days before Patrick replaced those baleful thoughts. The light was not good but I sped as fast as the child I carried would let me, praying for luck and safe passage. I would have neither, but the latter was my chief problem. The roads were sodden and dragged at my boots and my skirts, and though it was still afternoon, the clouds robbed me of light as I picked through the woods, imagining the sound of the river, a folly, to be sure, as it was of course clogged with ice.

The field became an incline, and I staggered through shifting drifts of snow, reaching for bare trees as one would a stair rail. It was slow, ponderous going, and my belly gurgled with the need to relieve myself. Not wanting to stop, but unable to contain the pressure the child made against my innards, I found myself debased on the hillside, covered in piss, my hair unsticking from its tidy cap in an unseemly sweat. Praying the river woman would have seen worse than the likes of me beseech her for aid, I grabbed for a bit of brush to steady myself. But the brush was not secured by roots, just a dead stick snarled in the snow and I tumbled headlong, boots over my ears, my belly seizing in terror even then of jeopardizing its cargo, and I heard, then felt my left leg snap like a clap of thunder inside my head.

+

+

+

What came next is only tattered. I cannot piece it correctly for the telling, as I was not inside my own self when it occurred. I was found, yes, and rescued. Mules dragged me by cart, a doctor was brought, my leg was fractured, the ankle swelling unnaturally.

I was miles from the river woman, in any event, and even she couldn't be enlisted for healing. I remember nothing of this, only caught it in bits later. Only the birth of our child I recalled. There was no medicine or herb that could give me reprieve from that feeling. Flesh twisted and ripped. Urgency, blood. Upon hearing the babe's cry, I went beneath the Holy Mother's veil, numb and blind to the suffering she knew so well, and when I woke again, I was miles from the Ganey farm, strapped to a cot in the cool marble palace where Maude and Arthur sent me to heal. Or so the doctors said. Healing was far down the list of wares that place had on offer. But it would be a while before I would come to sample their offerings—the haze of draughts, the misery of the baths—and so my first memories of the marble palace were of sleep, wails, and shouts seeping into dreams of Patrick, laced with the cries of our child, whose face I had not seen.

When I became upright, I was allowed water and soap. The baths were not just for washing, the nurses explained, but to cleanse me of ill thinking. I washed and streaked my wrists with the bottle of perfume one of the other women near me kept; it was a gift from a sweetheart, she would say, morning to night. When they took her away one afternoon, thrashing and shouting, I crawled to her cot and found the bottle, tucked in her sheets. It was milk white and smelled of lilies of the valley. I missed my home. I missed grass and dirt and the smell of dried linens on the Ganey farm. I missed Bess and her hands coasting through my hair at bedtime. I missed Patrick, the knot at his throat I had loved to kiss.

I stole the bottle. I warmed it between my palms after the lights were turned out. I hid it between my breasts, my thighs. When the perfume spilled one evening, I cried. But I kept the bottle, nonetheless. I owned nothing in the marble palace. My boots and dresses were locked in an attic, the nurse said. When I was remade whole, I could have them all back. I was allowed only a Bible and a crutch. My leg was heavy and slow to heal. I was encouraged to step lightly, to walk across the rooms as much as I could. But it ached and swelled, as did my breasts, which leaked milk every night until the nurse chided me for spoiling my sheets and bound them with herbs to stop the flow. I stood, holding the perfume bottle, while another nurse wiped milk and the scent of flowers from my skin. Then I was given a cup of tea and sent to another part of the marble palace. I woke days later and was told to write letters to my husband and sister-in-law. I snapped the pencil in half.

Missus Ganey, you must curb your temper, they said. *Write your letters, or we shall take your treasure.* Meaning the empty bottle. I did not destroy the new pencil. I wrote two letters, asking after the farm and Maude's health and Arthur's cattle. I described the view out of the window, which was of summer rioting to life, wide lawns fringed with trees, streams of honeysuckle clambering up trellises, women walking slow and stiff, steps ahead of their minders.

I did not ask after Patrick. I did not explain the pain in my leg. I did not wonder about the child I'd left behind. I had not left the child, after all. They could write their own story of this, later. The thought of it made me want to snap the second pencil. Instead, I asked the nurses for a book. I was given the Bible. I did not touch it. I asked for a needle and thread. They would not comply.

Weeks later, I watched a girl who did not speak any language I could recognize sewing daisies on the hem of her skirt. She used threads from her own bedding and the napkins from our meals. At night she picked at the hems of her skirt, her pillowcase, her pinafore; she rolled threads around her fingers like spools. When I could walk again, it was nearly the end of summer. Maude nor Arthur wrote me a letter, though I was made to write each week. If my letters did not suit the nurses, they were burnt and I was made to rewrite them. I could not tell of what happened as a matter of course in my days. The hot, strange teas, the long, blurry slumber they caused, the pokes of needles filled with clear poison. And once the plaster removed from my leg, the first stirrings of the water cure: wrapped in sheets, shivering in water cold as an icy spring, counting as the spokes of the clock moved like spider's legs. If I screamed, more poison needles. If I cried, nurses choked tea down my throat. I resolved to become as cold as slate. As icy as the water from the rusting taps in the baths. I willed myself to become clear poison, invisible ink, to dissolve under the arctic water, a strange bird plunging into the depths.

When the girl who sewed daisies went home with her chaperon, a great, heavy man with a pile of gray hair and a mustache like soot, I shook out the linens of her abandoned bed and found the needle. I stitched it through the thick skin of my arm and kept it there until the lights went out for sleep. Then I slipped my hand beneath my pillow and found my empty bottle. The clatter the needle made when I dropped it inside the glass felt like a sin.

The marble palace was a place of doors and chairs and noise. Nurses who sniped and pinched and bothered. I limped through the hushed halls with their smooth floors while wails echoed around me. I watched for dropped handkerchiefs and frayed curtains, stealing how the girl with no language had shown me. When it was found that my theft made lace and clusters of stars on the edges of my pinafore, I was given real thread, a hoop to embroider with, a stuffed doll that wanted for a dress. Nurses murmured how the stitch work calmed me and plied me with requests: a scalloped collar, a reticule decorated with honeybees, a set of dishcloths labeled for the days of the week. The letters to the Ganey farm were forgotten. I became a queen bee in a hive of homespun delights, all for the nurses to squeal over and spirit away as gifts to their families. My hands were sore and I begged for thimbles, which I kept in the pockets of my skirts. These announced my entrance to a room like a ghost's fetters. Nurses beseeched me to mend pockets, decorations for their caps. Shaking my thimbles, I asked for a pencil. I vowed not to snap it. I want to write my sister, back home across the water.

The doctor forbids it, they said. *Your mind must be calmed. Think of better times.*

Better times: beneath Patrick's body. My mouth soothed by his tongue. His hands warming me with plans and dreams. I never thought of our child, but I hoped he had returned to look upon him. I knew it was a boy. I did not learn what Maude named him.

In autumn, a new cast was set, one made not of plaster but of ritual. Beyond the drugged sleep and the needlework, my life was all baths. Each morning and evening, the doors to the bathing parlor closed heavy around me. The nurses would lead me inside, strip me of my shabby night rail and wrapper, swaddle me in cold sheets, submerge me in a tub so warm the shock of it made me feel faint. I could have stood that, but was required to finish with a frigid soak to chill my brain, the dark humors of my body. Nurses pressed me to undress. I learned there would be no profit in disobedience. Baring my skin to them, I sunk heavy into grief, into the water. The water gave shape to my days: the before, the after.

All Saint's Day I received a letter. Maude Ganey's stiff script. No word of Arthur, nor the child. Simply that she wished me well and had fond memories of sewing each night in the parlor. And that Patrick had disappeared. Lost, dead? She did not say. He had never returned to the Ganey farm. I should not carry false hope, she explained. I should pray for health, and better days. There will always be a place for you at our home, she said.

That afternoon, before my bath, I wrapped the wet sheets around me until my lungs protested. *Tighter,* I told the nurse.

For my health. For better days ahead. For forget-me-nots crushed under my heels as I ran across the fields to the arms of one I would never see as long as I remained on earth.

Chapter Nineteen

They ate pancakes and bacon at the kitchen table, all of them lavishly drinking orange juice or coffee with cream. Wade insisted on using real plates when Poppy found a stack of paper ones in the cupboard.

"Pancakes are fucking messy," he explained. "At least the way I eat them is."

"Wade's a Messy Jessie," Lilah said, and asked him for the cream.

"Slobby Bobby," Daisy added, pleased by the smile from Lilah. For a while, it was quiet but for the sounds of forks clinking and cups being set down and refilled. Hugh only drank coffee at first, his eyes red and weary, but finally stacked four cakes on top of each other and frosted them with melting butter.

"Hand me the syrup," he said. Daisy's and Lilah's eyes met, expecting Poppy to explode. Bad table manners infuriated her.

"Please?" he added, looking at everyone as if he was in a hurry, and Daisy was surprised that her sister merely handed the jug to Hugh and said nothing.

Thunder growled outside. Daisy cut her pancake into half-moons. She had slept terribly, but at least hadn't had more of the weird dreams from the other night.

Wade sorted through the bag of stuff from Walmart that Poppy had left on the counter, holding up various items. The coil of tubing, the bottle of castor oil. A speculum that Poppy must have stolen from Carna in his huge hand made Daisy startle.

"So, this how an abortion from the olden days goes, huh?" Nobody spoke. Hugh shook his head as if this were the real breach of etiquette.

"Basically," Poppy said, sighing. "Some of it's the same kind of thing you use for natural childbirth."

"What does that mean, even?" Wade asked.

Poppy ripped a paper towel from the roll Wade had set in the middle of the table. "You're basically trying to bring on labor," she said. "A lot of women do that, still. Women have done it for thousands of years."

"To get rid of the baby?"

"No, sometimes it's because the mother is tired of being pregnant, is overdue. There weren't always ultrasounds, you know. A woman would get weary after forty-five weeks of carrying around a baby. So, a midwife or someone else—a mother, an aunt—would do things to try to encourage the baby that it was time. To get the uterus to start contracting, really."

"Oh."

"In Lilah's case, she doesn't like pills."

"I hate swallowing tiny things," Lilah confirmed.

"You hate modernity," Poppy told her, sighing again. Daisy laughed, unable to help it.

"I took the fucking things, didn't I?" Lilah's voice was all venom. But her cousin ignored her and continued. "Some of that is just trying to bring on a regular period; some of it's to extract the uterine lining. That's something women would also do, too. If they didn't want another child, if it was too soon, they already had a little baby to worry about. It's the same process. The contractions—the cramps, if you're not pregnant—expel the contents of the uterus."

Wade's face screwed up uncertainly.

"Dude, you're the one who asked," Hugh said, downing his coffee.

"But why did you want to go to the hospital last night?" Wade pressed.

"Because," Poppy said. "I wasn't sure if what was happening was okay."

"What *was* happening?" Wade asked.

"Dude," Hugh said. "Really?"

"I realize you're not going to be as comfortable with a toilet full of blood," Poppy said, sitting back from her plate. "You don't see that every month like we do. But basically, that's what it was. But it just . . . It scared me."

"I felt super crampy, that was all," Lilah said to Wade. "They hurt, cramps."

"Even I knew that," Hugh muttered.

"Even Hugh knows that," Poppy said to Lilah. "I bet Hugh'd take Advil if he had cramps."

Daisy laughed again, but then held back. She was going to spit all her food across the table if she wasn't careful.

But Wade was stuck on other details. "Your toilet's full of blood every month?"

"Not all at the same time," Poppy said.

"Well, sometimes," Lilah said, her face still glum. "A house full of women tend to sync up."

"Not as much," Poppy said. "I bet this year was different, while I was gone. Plus my mom's in perimenopause."

"She is?" Daisy was surprised.

"Okay, but why the hell would a woman get pregnant when she already had a little baby?" Wade asked. "Like, isn't that the kinda thing you wait a little bit for? To, like, recover down there and everything?"

"You couldn't just tell your husband to get off you, back then," Lilah said. "It was his right, his wife."

"That why you picked Ty Haytch, then?" Hugh asked.

"Fuck off," Lilah said, sitting up straight now. "I didn't pick him. And I didn't pick this."

"You didn't use any birth control, though," Hugh said. "And we're not living in the old days now."

"You," Poppy said, her voice bright and deadly, "need to shut the fuck up. Right the fuck now."

Wade was quiet, but his eyes never left Poppy's. A flare of panic rose in Daisy. Would he tell, now? Would it all come out?

"If you must know," Lilah said, her voice wavering as it rose, "I always used something. With every guy. But one of them, he didn't put it on right. Or it was defective. Because it broke. At least that's what he said. Maybe he took it off. I'm not sure. It wasn't fun, if that's what you're thinking."

"You don't have to explain all this now," Daisy said. "It's not his business."

"Our mothers are always so dumb about this stuff," Lilah said. "It's not their fault. But they are. Carna acts like it's a tragedy and she's there to mop up the damage. Violet says it's all about joy. Finding joy in this life. She told me I needed to find my joy. So, I did."

She turned to Poppy, who was shocked and still. "It wasn't so easy, having you get all the attention in the whole school, and be me, the weirdo. So, when you were gone, some of the people you always told us were awful? They were nice to me. Kind. Fun."

Poppy's eyes stuck to her syrupy plate. "Don't even say it. I don't want to know."

"I will never say it," Lilah said. "Not to someone who doesn't want to know. Not to someone who just wants to judge me. Though I suppose all of you will anyway."

"I won't," Daisy said.

"Thank you," Lilah said. She stood, pushed in her chair. "That was a nice breakfast, Wade. I'm going to lie down now."

When Lilah left, Daisy felt strangely grown-up. Rarely was she left with the older ones like this, to sort through the wreckage with everyone else. She had always been the one everyone wanted to leave so they could talk about what mattered.

"You think she's into one of them guys?" Wade asked.

"I hope not," Poppy said. "But it's highly likely."

"Lucky for Haytch, I don't feel like doing shit today," Hugh said. "Because that fucker is a prick. And I could knock his ass in the dirt and not feel one bit bad."

"She never said it was him," Daisy said.

"Think about it, though. Who breaks condoms?" Wade asked. "Idiots who don't know how they work. Who's an idiot who knows nothing about condoms? Fucking Ty Haytch, my dumb-ass cousin, who thought you could get AIDS from a goddamn urinal in a gas station."

"He's the same guy who thought it wasn't a sin if you jerked off but didn't come," Hugh added.

"God," Poppy said, taking her plate to the sink. "I can't even hear this about him. Or anyone. Is this dishwasher dirty or clean?"

"Dirty," Wade said. "Just leave it there. You gotta know how to put everything in there or else it doesn't get clean. My uncle was supposed to fix it a while back, but obviously he's a real busy guy."

"Your uncle's not that bad," Hugh said, putting the orange juice back in the fridge. "I mean, he's kind of pathetic and whatever, but he's funny to get drunk with."

"I wouldn't know," Wade said. "Last time I drank with him, he tried to put me in a fireman's carry and then pissed himself."

Daisy laughed. Poppy looked like she might smile, but then she thought better of it and frowned.

"What are we going to do all day, then?" Hugh asked. "Just sit around and wait for Lilah's baby to fall out of her?"

"Stop calling it a baby," Poppy said. "It's barely an embryo."

"You hope," Daisy said.

Poppy wiped her hands on a dish towel and then smelled it, frowning. "Maybe you should wash this, Wade."

"So, housework," Wade said, standing up and stretching. "My dad'll be suspicious if I keep cleaning up this dump. He'll wonder what in the hell went on when he was Texas."

"We could watch more episodes of *The Reavers*," Poppy suggested.

"Fuck that shit," Wade said.

"That show sucks balls," Hugh said. "But I gotta lay down again. Your uncle busted out the Jäger bombs last night."

"Idiot," Wade said.

"I know, I know. Can you get me a bunch of Advil, D-Rock?"

"It's in the kitchen above the sink," Wade said. "Get it yourself."

"Aww, man, come on! I feel like nine kinds of ass!"

"At least you're not having a homemade abortion," Daisy said.

This time Poppy laughed out loud.

Chapter Twenty

I disliked Maude. I dislike her memories. But I feel a love for her that I cannot explain. She outlived Arthur by a decade; I witnessed some of her happinesses, which is soothing. And while I see the trap of Arthur's life, I do not feel the depth of the ache for him that I do for Maude. Perhaps this is in relation to how shabbily I treated her in life. She treated me equally poorly, yes, in many ways. All of this seems petty and small now.

The ache for Maude is there because her memories, unlike Arthur's, were private, secretive, incomplete. Once Arthur's desires became clear to him, the path forward was plain, though surely hidden from most others he knew.

Maude was different. She was a sister to me in ways neither of us would ever know.

✦
✦
✦

As a child, Maude loved the water. Unseemly for a young girl on a farm staffed with ill-bred men; I could only guess her mother's censure is what drove her to become secretive. Her own mind kept these thoughts close. It was fortunate that I have an abundance of time to work out the plumb line of the remembrances that plagued her.

First, there was her body. Big as Arthur's, then bigger than him. Her mother unsmiling as she fitted her daughter for a dress, watched her struggle to fit her broad hands into the kidskin gloves that had been a Christmas gift. This discomfort sent Maude to wash in the evenings, toward whatever private brook or pond she could find, seeking to flee the dismal view of her mother.

There is only one memory of her enjoyment of this. It may be that night washing was cold, or frightening. It may be that it was precious. I only know what came next: Maude was found out.

Shivering Maude, wrapped in her cast-off skirts, her lips blue with cold under the unseen man's lantern. Downcast eyes. He speaks soft and sweet. She follows the lamp beyond the pond toward where the barn would be built; at the time it was naught more than a few fence posts. Where she went, I couldn't know. Some memories aren't meant to be saved or savored. I couldn't sort out which the invisible man with the lantern had given her.

What came next: Maude's courses stopped. She was just sixteen and the first blood had come upon her one year previous. She goes out at night, in light of only a candle, to tell the man what has occurred. The man laughs. I hear the laugh; it is ugly and cruel. I hear him speak, just the once.

God curse whatever beast you bear, he says. And then he is upon her, pummeling her breasts and belly, until she's crumpled on the floor beneath him. He raises her skirts, swift. The memory ends there.

When I think of this, I want to cry out: *I am sorry for it, Maude! I am sorry, I did not know. I am sorry you had to carry that violence in secret, in loneliness. I am ashamed of myself, how I viewed her as spiteful only for the sake of spite.*

The next memory comes in winter. Maude is ill. Her mother is abed with another child that is taking its time in coming. Arthur waits until their father is asleep in the chair outside the room where his wife labors and takes Maude under his arm. He has a readied horse tied by the road; he places Maude atop the saddle and himself behind it and though he is a bad horseman, he brings them to a trot as best he can with only the half-moon's light. The trip takes an hour, perhaps more. Maude holds a lantern against her belly and the oil inside it sizzles. She wishes it would cure her of the ill inside her, that it would burn and scour out whatever is slowly dying within. She closes her eyes and tries not to lean against her brother; he is doing his best to keep the horse swift and on course so she cannot disturb his balance. She does not ask him how he knows about the river woman, what he did to arrange this. She has known about the river woman since she was a girl. She had pictured a witch making potions and spells, a woman stewed in her own wretchedness and evil.

The river woman's hut is smaller than Maude's mother's chicken run. There is a lantern on the gate; she is expecting them, as Arthur said she would be. She blows out the lantern flame when they dismount. The unseen river behind the hut struggles and moans beneath the ice.

The river woman is not beautiful. She is taller than Arthur, tall as Maude. Her face is not lined; she is young, this woman. Her hair is hidden beneath a dirty cap. She is missing some of her teeth, but she smiles at them kindly as she ushers them inside. *Why is she smiling?* Maude thinks. *She must not have a mother like mine. Or a mirror.* But then the river woman eases her toward a twisted chair by the hearth and Arthur hands the river woman a pouch of what must be coins. The chair creaks beneath her aching body. The river woman offers Maude a steaming cup and entreats her to drink.

Gather more brush, she tells Arthur. *Then go away from here and return come dawn.*

I will not leave my sister, he says.

This is your choice, she says. *Bring me the horse blanket before you collect the brush.*

Maude drinks from the steaming cup. It tastes like fire. Clay and coals and pitch. Her lips twitch in disgust but she drains the entirety. Whatever horror is inside her requires equal strength to defeat. She watches her brother return with the horse blanket and reclines on it at the request of the river woman. All night, she dreams and closes her eyes while Arthur feeds the fire and the river woman lifts her skirt, pressing on her belly, doing more things that hurt, holding Maude's hands as she cries.

We must go soon, Arthur presses. Dawn is near.

She cannot go yet, the river woman says. She would not survive the journey.

Yes, I will, Maude thinks, as something thick within her shifts and rushes between her thighs. I will.

✦ ✦

✦

Maude in the parlor, the same place I had sat beside her evenings and sewed. She does not sew. She will not sing or recite poetry or learn French. She is wearing black, for her mother has died months ago, delivering a stillborn babe, and the family still mourns. The mirror her mother loved to preen before is shrouded in hastily dyed crepe. It is spring, at last. The burial is this morning; her father has invited everyone they know, including a man he hopes Maude will marry. Though the sun shines and the fields around the house are blooming with life, she will not greet this man nor any other guest. She spreads a hand over where her black skirt meets her starched white shirt. Her mother's child was killed with its own cord noosed about its neck; her mother's womb worked to expel the dead baby for hours until she lay in a lake of blood. Their father ordered the cook and midwife to scrub the room with lye and steaming water, but Maude can still smell the odor of death. She thanks God for what the river woman wrought, and for the knowledge she lent that morning as Maude trembled out the gate toward her brother and the horse:

'Tis a pity, but I fear no babe will ever catch inside you again, madame.

'*Tis a pity*, Maude agreed. She thanks the river woman, though she knows her brother paid her. She knows it's not a pity.

It is a protection, as good as if the river woman bespelled her with a curse. She does not know it then, but she will never bleed between her legs from this night at the river woman's. She stands before the covered mirror, thinking of this luck that she cannot bear.

Only when Arthur calls her outside, saying the priest has arrived, does she leave the parlor.

Chapter Twenty-One

W ade did laundry. Hugh ordered a pay-per-view movie about cops raiding a skyscraper, and Poppy fell asleep. Lilah woke from her nap and requested *The Reavers* be put on. Daisy found a cabinet of games and laid out a board of Sorry, which she knew Poppy loved. While season three of *The Reavers* played along in the background, she, Hugh, Poppy, and Wade slapped cards on the board, screeching in outrage whenever someone sent their tokens back to start. Lilah went to the bathroom frequently, her face tight and worried, Poppy's glance following her until she returned indicating she was fine.

Around two o'clock, Poppy called Carna but got voice mail. She left a long message explaining that they were going into Hogestyn and would be home later. Daisy couldn't bring herself to look at her phone, even though it was fully charged, courtesy of Wade. She curled beneath the fleece blanket with Lilah and watched as the pirate brother in *The Reavers* was being tortured in some dungeon in Antwerp for stealing diamonds his sister-lover needed to fund her expanding couture shop in Amsterdam. Around six, Wade and Poppy went into town and bought groceries for dinner. When the rain finally let up, Hugh went out back to light the grill and Daisy went with him.

"All these firecrackers got wet," she said, bending over to the box of Black Cats.

"They're shit anyway," he said, stuffing a wad of dip into his mouth and running the scraper brush over the cooking grate.

"I hate fireworks," she said. "At least these kind aren't too loud."

"You're my half sister," he said. "Do you realize this, Daisy?"

"More like a cousin."

"What's the difference, especially in your family?"

Anger rose up without warning. "Oh, fuck you, Hugh." She bent over and picked up spent Black Cats.

"No, listen to me," he said, coming nearer, the grill brush in his hand. "We're as bad as those dipshits in that TV show."

"They don't do it until season four and besides, they're not really related, if you keep watching."

"I don't care!" he said. "The problem is that you can't think that this will go anywhere."

"Why would you think I would?" she said. "Because isn't Hugh Isherwood every girl's dream?"

"I didn't say that," he said. "We're a family. Even if it's totally fucked up and I could kill my dad for being such a cock, you can't have some little crush on me."

She threw the handful of wet Black Cats at him. He tried to duck but several of them hit him in the neck. One stuck to his T-shirt.

"I never, ever did anything to make this happen!" she said, her voice lowering to a rasp. "It was you who started it."

"Yeah?" he said, his voice joining her at the low register. He swatted firecrackers off him. "Who came over yesterday? Just walked in the door like she owned the damn place?"

"You could have told me to leave," she said. "You could have done lots of things."

"So could you."

"But I didn't want to leave," she said. "Unlike you, I didn't feel bad about it. Until right now, when you're acting like I'm going to start following you around, writing love notes or something."

He turned around, scraped the grill, and then chucked the brush onto the picnic table with a bang.

"I don't know how to fuckin' do this, okay," he said. "I'm the one who thought Poppy and me were such a great idea. And look what's happened there."

"Nobody asked for any of this, *Hugh*," she said, hating his name in her mouth. "People just do things. Or have things done to them. Nobody plans this. Your mother didn't plan to get hit by a cement truck—"

"Fucking don't bring her up," he said, his wrist over his eyes. "Just don't, all right?"

"But you're acting like it's all some crazy idea that I had, or my sisters had," she said. "If we knew the whole story, maybe it might make more sense. If we asked my aunt and your dad . . ."

"You want to ask them? Because I don't."

"It would probably help."

"Help what?"

"Help everything," she said. "The whole world isn't how it seems. You and Poppy are half siblings, and Wade has no idea that girls bleed into the toilet every month. And I didn't know that first-hand, myself, until this summer. I got my period the day of your mother's funeral. That time up in your family's barn? That was the first one."

He squirted chew out the side of his mouth, a perfect shot into the stack of firewood by the picnic table. He looked her body up and down, like he hadn't seen it before.

"Aren't you kind of, you know? Old for that?"

"I'm fifteen," she said. "What difference does it make?"

"Makes a lot of difference, knowing I'm nineteen and could go to fucking jail for touching you. Which is another reason you can't say anything."

"God, you're so fucking mean, you know that?"

"Daisy," he said. "I'm not trying to be mean. But I think you don't know as much about this shit as me. I've had lots of girl-friends. And girls that I did shit with. And they all act . . . They don't get it, sometimes. They think that something means some-thing, when it doesn't. Or they can't face that whatever the some-thing was, that it was just for that one time. Not forever."

Daisy crossed her arms over her chest. She was sick of wearing these same clothes and wished she could shower.

"I know it's not forever," she said. "I know, okay. You giant asshole! But it was my first time. So, thanks for making me feel like total shit about it!"

Before she could change her mind, she turned and sped down the Dunedins' driveway, past Wade's uncle, who was sitting in his lawn chair drinking a can of Hamm's, and down through the shelterbelt toward her house. Hugh shouted after her, but she leapt over fallen logs and thorny briars, past puddles and patches of dead grass and bits of tree bark with dead moss clinging to it, running until she got to the Ruin, where she slowed, catching her breath so she would appear normal to Carna and Violet when she came home. She wished she had thought of some better way to handle Hugh besides running away like a child. She wished she had normal sisters, for once, who you could tell your secrets to and not feel like you were burdening them or asking for a lecture. She noted the fallen maple, still latched into place like a fallen ship's mast on the roof, and wondered whether the tarp had held during today's rain.

Carna's car was parked in the driveway, but Violet's was gone. Mr. Isherwood's truck was gone, too, but the flowers he had brought her aunt were splayed on the path toward the front step, petals crushed.

She went inside and called hello. No answer. She took off her shoes. Carna's midwife suitcase was opened on the living room floor, her thermos on the coffee table. She went into the kitchen to pour a glass of water. It was strangely cool inside, the day's rain clearing away the summer's heat. She drank and set the glass on the counter. There was a bowl of strawberry hulls in the sink.

"Daisy?"

Carna, coming in from the back porch. She wore a shirt of Violet's, a slight halter top, the edges frilled in lace and dotted with little yellow flowers, and what had been a skirt Poppy made in tenth grade, a faded red embellished with green ribbon on the hem. Her legs were bare, a bruise on one knee; the old cloth from the chest upstairs that Poppy had been ironing was folded over her arm.

"You're all back? Where are your sisters?"

"They're coming in a bit," she said.

"How was the Fourth?"

"Fine. Where's Mom?"

"She went into town to get some food," she said. "We're having some people over this evening."

Daisy nodded, like this was routine. But Carna never wore skirts, never wore anything frilly. "What are you doing with that?"

Carna held out the fabric like a scroll. "Just looking at it," she said. "It's strange. It's like someone was trying to make a pattern. See? It's been pricked with a needle, I think. Like some kind of code. But it's not all the same. And it's so tiny, look. It's like another language, from another time."

"That chest was pretty old," Daisy allowed. "Must have been part of the original house."

"The original house was a stable," Carna said. "Evie told me about it years ago. If you look at the original walls, you can kind of see it."

Daisy had never been in a stable. No one she knew had horses, except for Gretel Coughlin, who had taken lessons in middle school.

They sat on the sofa, examining the cloth. The little holes were hard to see at first; some were sharper than others, as if different-size needles had been used. Daisy liked the way the cloth felt under her fingertips. Slight, but stiff, a map whose outlines she couldn't see.

"Was this the only thing in the chest?" she asked.

"No, there's more stuff in there," Carna replied. "Some clothing, though it's very damaged. A pair of boots. Sewing things."

Daisy ran up the stairs, where the chest had been moved to make way for the tarps. On the floor beside the chest was a head-board painted with peeling flowers. She opened the chest—it was heavy and rusted around the hasp—and saw more folded piles of yellowing fabric, the rotted boots, a flour sack that held wooden spools of thread and a tiny bottle with a stopper, the kind that might have held perfume. She opened it and sniffed; the cork was rotted and there was nothing but a clinking sound. Needles.

She brought these things down to Carna and they spread them over the sofa and the coffee table, to better see everything, touch it all.

Chapter Twenty-Two

The needle. The cork. The empty bottle. My thumbs capped with tin until green rings bloomed on my skin. Bess, my mother, mad at the waters of Roscommon, bearer of the shame I carried to the marble palace where not one soul knew my history, Patrick and his devil's magic, all lost.

Nights of my own madness, pressing and poking, the ways of the old women in my village, picking out patterns of beauty they saw in their own gardens, in the midnight sky over the sea that lapped their land like thirsty dogs' tongues. Telling. Telling. Telling. The wind beyond the windows roared in storms. Cups of tea, fresh folded sheets, new night rails delivered by faceless charities to the likes of me, caught in that inn of mourning, I sewed even when I had no thread.

Telling. Telling. Telling.

Waves of words, punctures, threadless sutures. Who I had been. Who I could have been. My sister, Bess, gone beneath the water in panicked shame. My own body, an unintended gift, lifted out of the deep by hands that were strong and fine and meant to let me go.

Now the telling lies folded in a chest taken from another woman who slept beneath the roof of the marble palace as I did. A woman I did not know, whom the Ganeys would puzzle over—a strange name stamped in the fabric lining of the chest. A chest carrying the ebb tide of my minutes here as a creature of God. My girls pass beside it, bumping it with their hips, their bare pretty legs. A riddle of a time before, when the place where they sleep kept Patrick's horses. Ganeys' horses.

It pleased me to see Arthur Ganey live to be a man of nearly sixty years. His sister, a few more than this. Of Patrick's fate, I may only wonder. One night when the moon is dark, I may travel and bend an ear low to the ground for word of him, the sound of his laugh ringing out of another boy's chest. Perhaps he hides from me out of shame. Perhaps he found another and forgot me. We were so young, then, and I can only travel so far until dawn.

There were no more marriages in that house for twenty years, a span broken when the child I'd given them made his stake for a bonny girl with golden hair and crooked teeth, two counties away. I took pleasure in knowing that night, after the feasting ended and the music stopped, that when candles blew out, the house still glowed with love and pleasure. For what are we given this world? It cannot be only to sorrow and not know delight in each other.

Chapter Twenty-Three

Everything was different with Lilah in August. At first, Daisy did not trust this new sweep of mood in her sister. But Poppy got a last-minute job at the YMCA reception desk, filling in for a lady who had to go on bed rest, and suddenly the Whitsun house filled up with the sounds of Lilah laughing and making sloppy Popsicles with grape juice concentrate and her sewing machine juddering through stitches at all hours, and something about this happy, hopeful Lilah—minus a stomping, doleful Poppy—seemed too good to waste on mistrust. Every day, Lilah made grape Popsicles out of a kit she'd found at a rummage sale, and which she ate for breakfast, lunch, and dinner, the sticky purple all over her fingers and the countertops. She felt sorry for the workers toiling in the August heat and made more flavors of Popsicles for them, as well: passing out rainbow bouquets whenever they took a break from chopping up the dead maple or reshingling the roof. By the time the tall, grave-faced man who Rob Isherwood hired to remodel the upstairs bedroom arrived, Lilah was experimenting with coconut kiwi and raspberry peach. Violet liked to get a report from this grave-faced man each evening when he would pack up to leave; she would smile and collect the multicolored sticks while he explained his progress, as if to say, *Isn't she sweet?* Wade came over every other night, sometimes to say hello, and other times to grill Lilah portobello mushrooms and play Frisbee; Lilah was terrible at catching but could throw brilliantly.

Violet took the cut slabs of the maple tree and sanded down the tops to use as little stools for a firepit she wanted to build in the former chicken run. Carna, wary of any more natural disasters beyond the ones she encountered between the legs of her clients, warned of fires consuming them next. The plodding heat remained fierce, interrupted some days by violent rainstorms that caused alarm over the height of the river, which threatened the highway they took to Hogestyn. Sandbags went up, and the Isherwoods brought down water and shovels for the workers who fought to keep the road from being flooded. Violet, whose church took a few turns at sandbagging along the highway, joked about plagues and biblical floods; Carna even sometimes laughed, and drove with Mr. Isherwood coolers full of water and fresh loads of sand he'd gotten from Home Depot. Nobody asked Carna why she now wore the beribboned shirts Lilah made, or how sometimes she was gone unexpectedly and dropped off by what sounded like a big truck long after midnight. By mid-August, the water receded and the heat returned to unwavering thick temperatures in the upper eighties, but Carna's nocturnal hours continued.

When Gretel Coughlin at last returned from all her summer

occupations, she came over to see the new room in the attic. She walked around, looking at the new windows and the big wide closets, gushing all the way back down the stairs about how fantastic it looked. Poppy, smearing on lip gloss before she left for work, rolled her eyes at Gretel's excitement but said nothing. Daisy had been surprised that Poppy was not more bitter about this development, especially as it had come too late for Poppy to really enjoy it. But now it seemed Poppy had caught Lilah's lethargy and silence, while Lilah was bounding up and down the stairs to marvel over the new space, twirling and giggling and sewing riots of flowers onto the hems of her skirts. Poppy had very little to say about anything that happened in the Whitsun house and who it happened to. While the rooms were being built, Lilah—now more affectionate than ever—slept with her mother, and Poppy stayed on the sofa, clamping the pillow around her head and turning away from the room to face the couch cushions, as if she were trying to pretend she was somewhere else. Other than to sleep, she was rarely around. Lilah tried to save some meals for her, but soon it became clear that Poppy was getting her nourishment elsewhere; the plates under their foil cooled, then curdled in the heat. But even this didn't puncture Lilah's buoyancy. It was as if Lilah understood that what Poppy had done for her was the final payment of some kind, and now that her tab was settled. Though, truly, Daisy had no idea what either of them was thinking. Sleeping out on the porch on Carna's chaise was a kind of escape; she couldn't imagine sharing a bedroom again with her sisters. For the first time in a long time, she didn't care what they did.

"I think your house is cute," Gretel said. "It always reminds me of a fairy tale. A witch's cottage, in the forest."

"With a treasure chest in the attic," Lilah said. "Did Daisy show you what we found?"

Daisy watched while Lilah opened the chest and pulled out the strange clothing and sheets, the leather shells that had been boots. Gretel nodded but appeared bewildered by the random scraps. The Whitsun women all loved the mystery of the chest's contents; Violet had moved it right into the front hall. She walked into the room and beamed when she saw them looking at it.

"Imagine these beautiful things, coming to us from over an ocean," Violet said. "What an honor, to preserve them in our home." She had done a sermon about the treasure chest last Sunday, which had resulted in one of the congregants from the Hogestyn historical society approaching her to ask to see what was inside it.

"How do you know where they came from?" Gretel asked. "Who would just leave their things behind, inside an attic?"

Violet went on to speculate on the possible origins of the chest, and then she opened it to show Gretel how the fabric had been poked to make a design. Some of it is words, she explained, pressing Gretel's hand over a patch that said, in swirled script, *the dark water.*

"It's a story?"

"We think so," Violet said. "Carna got some cigarette ash on it and then we saw the outline of the words, like a connect-the-dots thing? But it's so old, the people at the historical society said not to touch it until they can come and take a look. I'm cheating, I know."

Violet nestled the fabric back into the chest and closed it with a soft thud. "They said the dark and the dry of the attic probably preserved it perfectly. When you open all these old things and expose them to the light—that's when things become complicated."

Gretel asked how the historical society people would preserve it—under glass?—and Violet mused over the various ways the items in the chest might be conserved.

Daisy never said that she had seen the fabric before, how she knew how the words had been made, the purpose of the white bottle. There wasn't a way to explain that, anyway. She had not dreamed of the woman with no face since the night they'd spent at Wade's house. Listening to her mother and Lilah talk to Gretel about the chest made her itch with restlessness. She didn't like to think about the woman or the fabric or what it all meant. She wished for the feeling in Hugh's room, when she was just her body, no thoughts, no questions.

Daisy was glad when Gretel's mother came to collect her. She was glad when Lilah drifted down the driveway and was picked up by a truck that whipped up a tornado of pale gravel. She was glad when Carna set two juice glasses on the counter and poured one cup on ice for Violet, the other neat, for herself. Glad to hear her mothers push out the back door and wander the yard, past the empty chicken run, past the thick decaying garden where squash plants bolted through the metal gate.

Glad for the easy push out the front door and knowing the way to Hugh's. Glad for the wilted flowers that lifted their heads as the lowering sun dropped the temperature.

He had texted, and she had left soon after, the dead maple stump now filled with bright yellow mums Carna got from the woman who'd had the baby on the Fourth of July. On a sawhorse, the roofers' tools were covered by a faded white canvas.

Come to the berry field.

Okay.

Are you okay?

No.

Me neither.

He was waiting by the shed near the strawberry fields, unloading a bale of straw from the four-wheeler, when she arrived. The dead berry plants were yellow in the heat.

"What's going on?"

"Nothing," he said. "Just wanted to put the plants to bed for the year."

"You're going to open the patch up next year?"

"I don't know," he said. "My dad doesn't care either way. But if we don't set it up now, we're kind of already deciding, you know?"

She grabbed a rake from the side of the shed and began sifting through the plant rows, tossing dead straw into a pile. She had helped put the patch to bed that first year, but she had done it with Mrs. Isherwood and a few other kids, the radio on, mason jars of sweating cold water on an overturned bucket. And when they last did it, it was a late-September morning, cool weather for jeans—not hot August—with dark coming soon. She wondered whether Hugh knew that they could put this off for a while, but she didn't say anything. He seemed keen to work; his shirt was already dark with sweat. Some plants now looked too ragged to be saved, but she stooped over and cleared the sapped foliage so that Hugh could pitchfork fresh straw over it. By the time the light had mostly seeped beneath the horizon, he had run back for a third straw bale from the barn, but they hadn't even finished a third of the rows.

Rusty had ambled over by the time Hugh was ready to quit, nosing through the fresh straw, lifting his leg to pee wherever it struck his fancy. A sore on his back flank was raw and bleeding; Hugh kept hissing at him through his teeth to stop licking it.

"He's gonna get another goddamn infection, if he keeps dicking with it," he said, smacking at his dog with his ball cap.

"What happens if it gets infected?"

"It smells like ass and might get septic."

"Can't you take him to the vet?"

"Well, yeah. But he's almost fifteen years old, Daisy," he said. "He's lived outside his whole entire life. It's a miracle he's lasted this long, fussing at all his parts like he does. Brian always thought he'd be dead by the time he graduated. We're all amazed he's hung on this long."

As she did the math back from Brian's graduation, adding up the blessing of Rusty's extra years, the dog twitched away from Hugh's cap, sniffing down the last row they'd put to bed.

Hugh wiped his forehead with his shirt, and she stared at him without shame, admiring his pale belly slick with sweat. She had not heard from him since the time at Wade's. His hands were red from handling the straw, there was a swath of grease down his forearm, and he needed a haircut and a shower. But so did she. Her split ends were terrible, her chin was breaking out, and her sweat smelled so much more intense than normal; she wondered if she'd get her next period soon. Today Lilah had used up the hot water by the time Daisy came back from her morning trip down the ravine, so instead of waiting for the water heater to fill again, she put on yesterday's clothes with fresh underwear and a sports bra and knotted her hair into a ponytail. Her T-shirt and shorts were sweaty and spoiled, even the trails of denim thread on her thighs were now dark with dirt, and her arms dusty from her biceps to her blackened fingernails. She would have to rinse off before captain's practice tomorrow or she'd leave her to meet him, even if it meant She was glad Hugh had asked her to meet him, even if it meant getting filthy in the berry field. The fact that Hugh didn't seem to care about her crappy outfits or dirty hair was comforting but also a little weird. She kept waiting to become a person who cared about her appearance the way Poppy and Lilah did, but with someone like Hugh, who had known all of her body, in ways she hadn't known herself, this vanity didn't seem to be anything that might happen anytime soon.

"We'll finish tomorrow," he said, following Rusty down to the end of the row. "But go get that watering can and fill it up quick, will you?"

She did as he asked, careful not to scrape her hand on the sharp part of the metal can, and came to the end of the row, where Hugh was now spading up a particularly beaten-down strawberry plant, shaking the roots over the newly uncovered black dirt. He nodded for her to sprinkle the exposed part of the soil with the watering can, and she obliged. Then she set down the watering can and watched as Hugh dug. Rusty sat beside him, tail swishing aimlessly.

Once the hole was to his liking, Hugh pulled something from his pocket and knelt down. Rusty nudged closer, his nose sniffing at Hugh's hands, which held a tiny little blue bottle. He unscrewed the top and tipped it over the hole until a little plume of powder spilled out. Once the powder was gone, he tossed the bottle into the hole as well.

"See you next spring, Mom," he said, watching the hole for a long time. He finally looked up at Daisy with an uncertain smile. Though she might have said a multitude of things, Daisy chose to be quiet. He pushed the dug-up dirt over the hole and she knelt to help him, patting the mound of fresh earth with the same fondness she might pat Rusty. Then he splashed some water over the mound and looked down at it, his lips working like he wanted to say something more. But then they stood up and brushed themselves off and he started the four-wheeler, and together they roared over the fields, Rusty jockeying alongside them in joy, glad for the chance to chase, even if he fell back before they reached the barn.

He parked the four-wheeler by the duck pond, and then without warning or waiting, he splashed into the water, shoes still on. She followed him, shocked by the cold, the thick green water sour in her nose as she came to the surface. Rusty stood on the dock and wagged, refusing to jump in. After a while of treading water, they climbed out.

"I'll go get you a towel," he said, jogging toward the house, his shoes squeaking with water. Using a long stick, she collected her flip-flops, which had floated in two directions once she hit the water, and then squeezed out her ponytail. A thin wind rushed through her wet clothes in the dark, making her shiver. There were lights on at the Isherwood house, some faint noise from the television through the patio door. Rusty cantered around her, alternately twisting to chew the sore on his leg and nudging his snout into her hand for her to pet him. All around, fireflies introduced themselves and then vanished immediately after.

Hugh jogged back, barefoot, holding towels and a paper sack. She dried off as best as she could, and then, he nodded toward the barn. They rustled up the hayloft ladder, still dripping water, the paper sack clinking and crumpling, and sat by the hayloft door again, the night open in front of them, the only light from a curl of moon and the lone streetlamp that flickered on the corner of Old Blackmun Road. He opened a bottle of root beer for her and rolled down the sack so they could get at the peanuts.

She thought of many things to ask him. Were there more ashes from his mother? Where would they put them next? Had he noticed his father out with her aunt? Could she work for him next summer, if the berry patch opened again? Did he see now how much older she was, much older than the fifteen years she'd been assigned?

But she just cracked peanuts and drank root beer and looked out at the night dabbed with moonlight and fireflies starting their twilight business. Right now, she was glad for his company, his easy ways. Glad for any bit of promise this night could build between them.

Glad for the creases of black on his callused fingers. Glad for the meek drip of water from her snarly hair onto the old wood. Glad for the rustle of the paper bag, the snap of fingertips on peanut shells, the distinct clink of the brown bottles of sugary soda. Glad for the whisper of breeze that came through the hayloft door every few minutes.

"School starts up soon," he said, tapping her knee with his knuckles.

She nodded, gulped root beer.

"Are you excited?"

"Not at all," she said, sighing and shaking her head.

He smiled, and then they began to talk about everything else besides what had happened this summer.

Chapter Twenty-Four

God laughs at us. Though I was spared the memory of birthing Patrick's babe, our Lord granted me the grace to see our child die, cut down in only his middle years, clutching his chest beside the barn in midwinter, sinking to his knees, the frost coating him until the dogs' barking sounded the alarm to his family. Our boy, unnamed by me, took Arthur's name, but they always called him "Hughson" after their own father's name. He was beloved by many, at any event, the wake and burial lasting nearly a week, the music and drink flowing, the shouting and singing coming in great waves.

Since they buried him, I have watched the names course down over the years, the features of my sister and brother and mother. Of Patrick, too. Red hair, dark hair, freckled cheeks, swift hands, strong arms, sharp tongues, all sluicing down the chute, a family that had been my own, lost to me, and again become mine. The names wrapping around my kin, a rush of clans and crests. The Whitsuns, pushing forth without a man to carry the mantle, named for a feast only one of them marked; the Dunedin, far from their

Scotsmen in Dùn Èideann; the acid tongue of Haytch, wrought from the sly Haedesch, a name like a gunshot, or the snap of a rabbit snare; the Coughlins lacking the capes of the Ó Cochláin, and the Isherwoods, long way gone from Lancashire, their bright red barn still opening doors to whatever the future may bring.

It brings me no pleasure to say that ours was a beautiful child. But I msut say that, despite the sin of pride, despite the grief of never knowing him, holding him, feeding him from my own breast. I had not wanted him; he had been a guest uninvited into my body. Still, he was mothered by Maude and taught by Arthur, and fate would have that he drew in others, all of his days, until his destiny struck him down that February beside the old barn.

I drown in bitterness when I think of how his eyes gleamed. For this, I endeavor not to consider his eyes, nor his father's.

For solace and joy, I turn to my girls and their mothers. They are so clever! In them is my preferred drama, the ache and tumble of possibility, an abundance of care tempered with lashes of caution. I see the world as a place that might spread itself open, and the visage of my own sister calls to me from the deep, between this place and the place where we were born, the sun of her love desperate to touch me, the coolness of my time here tilting toward her. There is so much she would never know. Someday I may reach her.

But even amongst these girls, these women, there remain secrets. Wings fluttering between them. Distractions. The mothers' glances thick with wordless messages.

For the unicorn lass, there is a boy who keeps bits of her heart; he does not know he is one of many. Private conversations and longings stretch between them. Secrets, too. He does not know of how their fates were wrapped together inside her for a time. His mind lies trapped, like my name, in the Ganeys' Bible. Her mind is on the way his skin feels against hers, the despair of days when her mind convinces her body to stay buried beneath quilts, to seek out tears. She thinks of the babe she did not have; she ponders names late at night in bed, her eyes on the once-fractured seam in the ceiling. When I watch her, I find myself remembering what I cannot reclaim. It is the closest I can come to human pain now. I visit her dreams on occasion. Little Christmas. Midsummer. Those who remain must mark their own seasons.

The eldest palomino girl has left. Voyaged out to other places. I do not see her but for feast days. Her eyes have always been on the horizon, seeking what might be a better place to live. She carries ire close to her breast, always. There is something fierce in how she loves her sisters, and this scares her. I do not like to visit her dreams. There are battles and tears ahead. Clever like Maude, her mind a sleek contraption, always pursuing what lies just out of reach.

The youngest dark bay is the one whose dreams I like best. Her mind is rich, for she gives over her attention so wholeheartedly. She is stitched from curiosity. Like a dandelion clock blown into the wind, she moves through the dark toward the boy on the Ganeys' farm. What hums between them is not quite love, not quite lust, a tension that I cannot resist. In particular she specializes in surprises that make him laugh. The evening before last, I watched as the boy pressed his hand to her shoulder, her face, whispered words that would make Patrick Casey himself blush, and I regret never knowing our child, this boy's ancestor, as only a mother can.

As for the girl, she might yet learn what it is to be in this world. I cannot be certain where her feet will land, but I keep hope that she will remain near the place where she once played as a little girl, on the ruin where I became the creature I was allowed to be, then, honored and loved by the trembling hands of one who was just a boy himself, and now, known and revered by none.

Acknowledgments

So many people helped me through the writing of this book.

My husband's aunt Barbara Durand gave me the gift of the story to begin with, when she told me the family tale of how her ancestor, a fisherman named Patrick Murphy, pulled a woman named Jane Murphy from the Bay of Fundy, after her ship (full of Irish immigrants like herself) sank in a storm; they were later married and had many children. The rest of what happened to Jane Murphy in my story is a complete fabrication on my part.

The team at Penguin gave this book so much thought and care. Julie Strauss-Gabel provided a good loving home for the story; Melissa Faulner, Natalie Vielkind, and Anne Heausler helped these pages to read the way they should; Anna Booth and Samira Iravani designed the beautiful physical product; Naomi Duttweiler ensured that it found its way to readers. I have no idea how to do so many of these tasks and am so pleased to have them attended to by such good people.

Michael Bourret: thank you for being so supportive and loving to me, and for encouraging me to prioritize my family's well-being as well as my own. I am lucky to have you on my side.

Andrew Karre: you are a font of patience and delight. The

giddy joy we have together as a story rolls out is my favorite part of this job.

My mother, Karen Mesrobian, has always made history an intellectual and personal pursuit, in our family and her professional work. Writing a historical novel would have been impossible without the foundation she provided. Thanks, Mom, for giving me your curiosity.

Melinda Brown, Kari Fisher, Meagan Macvie, and Sydney Purdy: thank you for being year-round sounding boards and my favorite summer vacation.

Christa Desir and Sharon Biggs Waller: thank you for our rejuvenating winter retreat, your full-throated friendship, and keen writing insights.

My sister, Kristin, is an excellent person for a fiction writer to have as a sister. Thank you for weeding my garden and planting my flower beds and swimming laps and walking dogs and going to thrift stores and eating chilitos with me, all things I need to feel better in mind and body.

Adrian and Matilda: you make everything worth it. Thank you for being exactly who you are.

I was lucky enough to lay hands on *A Woman's Book of Choices: Abortion, Menstrual Extraction and RU-486* by Rebecca Chalker and Carol Downer. Thank you to Andrew Karre for securing me a copy. I hope that it will come back into print soon.

The following books were quite helpful in various aspects of research:

Barns of Minnesota by Doug Ohman

English As We Speak It in Ireland by P. W. Joyce

Erin's Daughters in America: Irish Immigrant Women in the Nineteenth Century by Hasia R. Diner

The Famine Ships: The Irish Exodus to America by Edward Laxton

The Graves Are Walking: The Great Famine and the Saga of the Irish People by John Kelly

In My Blood: Six Generations of Madness and Desire in an American Family by John Sedgwick

The Irish Famine: An Illustrated History by Helen Litton

The Irish in Minnesota by Patricia C. Johnston

Irish in Minnesota by Ann Regan

Mapping the Great Irish Famine: A Survey of the Famine Decades by Liam Kennedy, L. A. Clarkson, E. M. Crawford, and Paul S. Ell

Minnesota Farmers' Diaries by William R. Brown, 1845–46, Mitchell Y. Jackson, 1852–63

Of Irish Ways by Mary Murray Delaney

Ourselves Alone: Women's Emigration from Ireland, 1885–1920 by Janet A. Nolan

Stalking Irish Madness: Searching for the Roots of My Family's Schizophrenia by Patrick Austin Tracey

Tracking and Reading Sign: A Guide to Mastering the Original Forensic Science by Len McDougall

Wash and Be Healed: The Water-Cure Movement and Women's Health by Susan E. Cayleff